D1524082

To God, for Your blessings and protection.

In memory of my late Mom, the real Jo Ann.
She left this world much too soon.

The Ghostwriter and the Gems
(A Lighthouse Inn Cozy Mystery)

Jacqueline Sable

CONTENTS

ACKNOWLEDGMENTS

Thank you to all of the wonderful people who helped me with this book in many different ways. I'd like to thank the following people for their involvement: John Schertz, Jean Schertz, Tammy Willis, Michael Schertz, Rebekah Bryan, Gregg Voss, Veronica Foskett, Naomi Foskett, Heather Liban, Michelle Somerville, Chris Steiner, Michelle Renee, Kim Dussault, and Janell Madison. Many other people have been helpful with this book, especially since I decided to re-release it; I am very grateful to them all.

I'd like to give a special shout-out to Officer Joe Nichols of the Oshkosh Police Department, who answered some questions. I realize that I took some poetic license with the legal system, but this is a work of fiction and should be read as such.

Although I majored in English Literature, please realize that I am human and often err. If anyone catches additional errors, please feel free to email me at jacquelinesable.author@yahoo.com

And, I am grateful for the wonderful support I received while writing this book. To my family and friends, I owe you all a huge debt of gratitude.

Lastly, I'm so grateful to those who've read or are reading this book—especially those who have reviewed my little book. The positive reviews boosted my fragile ego and the negative reviews helped me grow as a writer. I would love to hear from my readers, so here are the ways you can connect with me:

If you like what you've read, please consider leaving a review. Also, please Like my Facebook page to receive updates https://www.facebook.com/RealJacquelineSable

And it would be great to connect with you on Goodreads too: Jacqueline Sable on Goodreads

Thank you.

PROLOGUE

AS THE MAN HUNG UP THE PHONE, he felt uneasy about the direction this whole operation had taken. He sighed heavily, sinking down into his leather chair.

"What did they want this time?" the gorgeous redhead asked as she handed him whiskey in a crystal glass. Only the finer things. And where had it gotten them?

The man ran his hands through his hair. She ignored this "tell" that indicated he was done with the discussion. He needed to talk about this recent development.

She hid her frustration as she pressed him. "They are asking unfair things of you. Why don't they leave you alone?"

"Because they have me over a barrel, Babe." He stood up and walked over to the window. As the owner of a vanity publishing company, he did all right. This apartment in downtown Chicago, his beautiful wife, and a fleet of vintage cars stood testament to his success. However, most people couldn't possibly know about his side job.

Now it was her turn to sigh. "So, what do you need me to do?"

"Just keep the home fires burning till I get back."

1

"Where are you going this time?"

"Door County."

"Door County? Why up there?"

"Marcos."

"Oh. Well, be careful."

"I will. I'm more worried about the help I have to bring on for this job." He ran his hand through his hair again and turned to face her.

"Help? Why don't you use the help you've used in the past?"

He grimly smiled. "You still don't fully understand the operation, do you? I can't use them—they are brutes. I need a lighter hand for this one. Someone who they would never suspect. Someone who appears above suspicion."

"You have to involve someone innocent?"

"I do, but they shouldn't come to any harm. Once the transaction is made, they'll be in the clear. They'll never know the part they played in this whole thing."

"So, who will help you this time?"

"One of the ghostwriters. I think I know just the one to do it. The patsy needs to be a bit naive, preferably a little dense."

"Most of your writers are pretty smart, aren't they?" She bit her lip in anticipation of his answer.

"Most are, but one is a bit of a ditz and not really the brightest bulb. She is very young and curious, but always seems to ask the wrong questions. Plus, all of her books have had to be rewritten almost from scratch."

"Annie Malone."

"Yes, Annie. This book isn't a real project. I just hope she doesn't figure that out."

Meanwhile, up in Door County, another phone was picked up.

"We got him," the agent's contact called him immediately. The publisher never even knew his phone was bugged. The agency had been watching the publisher for a few months.

"How?"

"He'll be bringing in someone new."

"Who?"

"Can't you ask me more than one-word questions?"

"Maybe when you start giving me real answers."

"I can't tell you anything now, but we should probably meet up."

"Agreed, but aren't you being watched?"

Ignoring this question, the contact asked, "Usual spot?"

"Will do."

CHAPTER 1

TOOTHPICKS.

Toothpicks would work, I thought, as I sat in the most boring meeting known to mankind. Tape, too. Tape would help hold the toothpicks in.

I felt my chin hit my chest, before it bobbed right back up. If I could just prop my eyes open with toothpicks, I figured at least I could look awake and get a nice little nap in on the sly.

I looked out the windows again in a feeble attempt to perk up. However, the grey autumn sky outside matched the grey walls in the conference room. Longingly, I watched the birds—envying them their freedom. But don't worry; this isn't THAT kind of story. My name is Joanna, er "Annie," Malone and this is the kind of story where a young woman (ahem, me) gets involved in a bizarre situation. But, I'm getting ahead of myself…

So, with the boredom of the meeting and the grey surrounding me, I worried that I'd be lulled into a trance. Oh no, did I just drool? Crap, I think I did.

"Annie, what is your opinion on the change control processes enabling the system to determine the root cause, therefore aiding in developing a synergistic approach?"

asked my boss, Karen Smith, jolting me back to reality. "And how do you feel about the qualitative measures needed for the assessment of the reallocation of the artifacts for the decomposition?"

I gaped at her in confusion.

"Annie?"

Of course, Karen did have my complete attention now. "Yes?"

Karen let out a huge sigh and repeated her question.

I blinked at her rather stupidly. I couldn't shake the paranoid feeling that Karen was torturing me on purpose. I knew I could not speak business gibberish. Each meeting I attended made me feel more and more idiotic. I figured by next year I'd be a mumbling mass of goo. When I graduated from college the year before, I hadn't expected the business world to be so business-y. I hadn't expected the grey drabness everywhere. Plus, I really hadn't expected the stifling suffocation that results from sitting in a cubicle. And when called upon in a meeting? I either froze up or overshared from nerves.

True to form, I squeaked out, "A-a-artifacts? You mean like in archeology?"

That, and my sputtering, really made me look like I didn't know how to actually do my day job. (I didn't. I had hit the Peter Principle pretty early in my probably-soon-to-be short career. One year and I hit the ceiling on job knowledge. Pathetic.) Rather than a marriage of convenience, I had a job of convenience, and it really fell short on convenience.

The hair on my neck prickled as I felt everyone's eyes on me. I knew I'd stepped in it yet again. I also knew Karen would descend upon me the minute the meeting ended. I knew that my face and ears were bright red. Despite being a brunette, I had unusually fair skin. Blushing easily betrayed me all the time.

On the upside, I thought, at least I'm not dozing anymore. Karen gave me a withering look, muttered something sounding suspiciously like "incompetent idiot" under her breath, and moved to the next topic.

As the meeting droned on, I simultaneously felt my eyes glaze over and my phone buzz in my front pants pocket. Ooo, a distraction!

I pulled my cell phone out of my pocket under the conference room table. The number on the display came from downtown Chicago, more specifically, from the editor for my moonlighting job as a ghostwriter. I wondered about the call and hoped he had a new ghostwriting project for me. The hit on the economy had made ghostwriting jobs harder and harder to come by. I had started writing for this vanity press in college. I had majored in English and writing books seemed like a natural progression. I'm still not sure how I got hooked into Quality Assurance documentation for my day job. The pay is great, but the job is drier than dirt and difficult for someone who got a D in Logic.

After college, I decided to keep ghostwriting in my spare time. What does this mean? Basically, I write stories for people who don't want to write for themselves. When people first hear what I do, they think it sounds oh-so-glamorous. They think that until I share some of my war (ahem, horror) stories with them, and the fact that I typically get the bottom of the barrel client-wise. No celebrities here. Plus, ghostwriting at my level doesn't pay the rent on its own. My editor, Harry Scarpelli, kept promising, "bigger and better things, Doll," but hadn't delivered yet.

Hence, the soul-sucking office job during the day.

Happy for the distraction, I slipped the phone back into my pocket and daydreamed about the potential of Harry's call.

After the meeting, I dropped my laptop back at my desk. Before Karen could catch me, I slipped down to the break room to listen to Harry's message.

"Annie, doll, you need to call me right away. I have a

project that's perfect for you. Be sure to call before seven tonight." Great. No details.

While it wasn't that unusual for Harry to not leave details, it would have been a nice change of pace, I thought as I saved the message. When Harry had a project "that's perfect for you," I had discovered it usually meant, "a project no one else wants" and "don't screw it up." I figured I'd call him back after work.

I turned to face the vending machines. My eyes dilated slightly at the sight of chocolate. I decided to indulge myself before my battle started with Karen. I knew the battle would begin soon—the chocolate was my meager attempt to arm myself.

"Oh, hi Miss Annie!" chirped my colleague, Tessa, as she entered the break room. "Whatever are you doing down here?"

The fakeness just dripped from her honeyed voice. Tessa was the bane of my existence at CritiCentric. She had stolen our coworkers' ideas more than a few times. Rumor also had it that she had played "mattress mambo" with the Vice President to get hired by the company. She tried to come off as a sweet person, by calling people "sweetie" and "honey." But no one really bought it, except the head of the department, Karen. When Tessa needed to strike, she did so with deadly accuracy. I trusted an alligator more than her (well, Karen too, for that matter).

"Hi Tess. What's up?" I said, resignedly.

"What was that display all about in the meeting?" Tessa sneered. "Cat got your tongue?" She cackled at her own joke.

She mimicked my squeak. "'Artifacts? Like from archeology?'"

I stood there silently, wishing for courage. A backbone was what I needed, I knew that. Somehow, the job had become more important to me than my own individuality, and I was upset with myself for that. I needed a change, but I didn't know how. And Tessa's taunts only made it worse. The guts to tell her off once and for all always failed me.

Stopping just short of sticking my tongue out at Tessa, I swept out of the room with as much dignity as I could muster.

"Wow, someone is rude," I heard Tessa say as the door shut.

Desperately, I wished—AGAIN—for the guts to stand up to Tessa and pop her in the nose. Well, maybe not actually hit her, but… well, I don't really know what. But her goading made me so upset.

I also wished for the guts to leave the corporate life behind. Cubicles and the lack of freedom they represented depressed me. It always struck me as odd that students got more and more freedom as they went through school. By the time I got to college, I managed my own time and space. Once I started working, others managed my time and dictated where I should be most of the time. I didn't know if others felt this way, probably not. *And I'm not ungrateful for my job. I'm grateful. I just think I picked the wrong profession for my personality.* Quality Assurance documentation was too dry and numbers-oriented for my liking. I enjoyed being around people and helping them.

Furtively, I scampered back to my little grey cell. I hoped to avoid the inevitable confrontation with Karen.

"Hey, Johanna!" Karen called to me. "Can you wait up a sec? I need to talk to you."

I knew all too well, why she needed to talk to me. After all, I had caused this mess. So consumed by my worries, I neglected to notice that Karen lugged three huge books with her.

"Sure, what's up?"

"Let's go into a conference room." Uh oh, Karen confirmed my fears. That's never a good opening for a chat with the boss. If it's good news, they might want to walk and talk, or they simply pop their heads into the cubicle for a quick chat. When they want to drag someone off to a room with a door that closes, it means they need to say something private and probably painful.

"What exactly happened during the meeting just now?" asked Karen. She looked at me with fascination, as if I were an exotic creature. That others didn't find Gantt charts and improvement processes amazing and wonderful seemed unfathomable to her. I suspected that Karen thought I was the worst kind of sinner—someone who did not really care about such things. I knew that Karen had told Human Resources she thought I was kooky. Karen's obsession with process reflected itself in her appearance. Always maintaining the ultimate professional composure, Karen styled her light brown hair in the appropriate pageboy and always wore neutral-colored pantsuits. I wore a bright pink sweater once, and she gave me the stink eye during our staff meeting.

"Wh-What? I'm sorry am I missing something?" Embarrassed, I refused to make eye contact. I figured the best defense was ignorance. Yeah, I figured wrong. Go figure.

"Well, when I questioned you in the meeting, your answer clearly showed you weren't paying attention. Now, either you don't understand what is needed of you, or you need to research the topic more. I'm going to assume it is the latter. Therefore, I am recommending that you read these books to learn more about system design processes."

And with that, she proceeded to drop three encyclopedic-sized tomes in front of me. *Boom! Boom! Boom!* The table seemed to sag a little under their weight.

"Karen, I understand you completely. I will get on these books as soon as possible. When do you need me to complete my research by?"

"Friday at 10 a.m. You will be giving me and Stan a 30-minute presentation on what you've learned."

Friday. My jaw dropped as I swiftly calculated. Today was Monday. My heart followed my jaw. Only four and a half days? And I did have a date tonight.

"All three books?" Darn it, there was that squeak again.

"Yes, or there will be consequences." Visions of pink slips danced in my head.

Karen had found my Achilles' heel: public speaking. My normally sunny demeanor diminished exponentially in ratio to the amount of people paying attention to me speaking.

In stunned silence, I walked back to my cubicle with the books. I wasn't quite sure what to do with the books. Should I take them home for some light night reading? Sigh. The incinerator seemed like a much better place.

•••

My apartment was in downtown Milwaukee on the corner of State and Cass. The area had some growth, but the mindset of the city seemed entrenched in a weird inferiority complex to Chicago. With this inferiority complex, the city had stagnated to the point of moving backwards. While I liked my apartment, I only stayed in the city for convenience. I had family fairly nearby, and I could walk to my job on Wisconsin Avenue. Plus, if I stood on the edge of my sofa and craned my neck, I could see a patch of Lake Michigan. Naturally, I paid for that lake view, but I loved being so close to the water.

On this night, I threw my brown Coach purse and black laptop bag on the couch, dropped the three books on the coffee table, and went to the kitchen for a drink. As I flopped onto my vintage (in other words, old, very used, and very free) easy chair, I grabbed my cell phone to call Harry back. The minute I touched the phone, it started ringing. I almost dropped it. Caller ID told me it was my Grandpa. I adored my Grandpa. Grandpa, also known as Frank Malone, was a retired cop, who lived with his sister, Helen Kravidocz, in a suburb of Milwaukee called Wauwatosa. Aunt Helen had moved in with Grandpa after Grandma had passed away. The move worked well for the widowed siblings—it staved off loneliness, and Aunt Helen kept Grandpa on his toes. It also kept Grandpa off my back, so it was a win-win-win.

"Hey Papa," I answered the phone. "How are you?"

"Hello! Better now that I've talked to you, Anna Banana." An old line, but one that always made me smile. "How are you? Are you coming home for dinner? Your Aunt Helen is expecting you." Even in a cheerful tone, his voice sounded a little growly. I shudder to think how many would-be suitors he had scared away with his low, bass-like voice when I lived at home.

Looking at the three books on the coffee table gave me pause. "Sorry, Papa, I'm not gonna be able to make it home tonight. How about tomorrow night?"

"Suit yourself. But remember to take it easy. Try not to burn the candle at both ends."

"Okay, Papa. I love you."

As we disconnected, I could hear Aunt Helen yelling in the background, "Well, can she make it for dinner, Frank?"

Smiling to myself, I pulled up Harry's number and hit "Send." As the phone rang, I wondered how on earth I was going to stay awake while reading the books Karen gave me.

"Hey doll." I rolled my eyes at his stock greeting for every female.

"Hey Harry," I said. "How are you? So, what's this 'perfect project'?"

"If I were any better, I'd be dipped in gold. Oh, this project is perfect for you, Sweetheart." I imagined him chomping on a cigar as he spoke. Sometimes it felt like Harry fell straight out of the sky from the 1960s. I thought he must be the personification of *Mad Men* meets the Elliot Gould character from *Ocean's Eleven*. I hadn't met him face-to-face yet, but I had high hopes that the image matched the man.

"In what way? Hmmm… ya know, that's what you said about the chick who wrote about robots being used during the Revolutionary War. She was a nut! She wrote the book for Liberace. Not as a dedication. He was her audience. And he's been dead for quite a while. I don't know how she thought…"

"Okay, okay. So, we haven't always given you the best of the best," Harry deftly cut me off. "But this! This is a great project. And we know you can handle this guy."

"Handle this guy?" All kinds of alarms went off in my head.

"Well, there is a catch."

I sighed. Of course, the inevitable catch. Nevertheless, my mind churned, this could be your way out of CritiCentric. Just hear him out.

"What's the catch, Harry?"

"He's got anger issues, Annie."

"Okay, define anger issues."

"Well, that's tricky…"

Tricky? The hairs on my neck bristled in warning. I covered the phone's mouthpiece and muttered, "I know I'm going to regret this." Louder, I said, "Harry. Focus. You want me to interview this guy. I need to know what to expect."

"Okay. Okay. Remember, you asked me to tell you. No one in the office wants to talk to him. I'm the only one he doesn't yell at."

Ignoring the comment about the client yelling, I asked what seemed to be a logical question, "So, why don't you take the project?"

"Doll, I have my hands full. Plus, I know that you have experience with handling difficult people. You interview people really well, really dig into who they are. And I figured with your sweet nature…"

"Sheesh. All right, cut the crap, Harry. I need this project, so I'll probably do it. What does the gig pay?"

"Twenty thousand dollars." My phone slid from my hand as my vision dimmed a little. Through a fog, I could still hear Harry talking as I picked up the phone.

"I'm sorry, Harry. I've had a really bad day and don't think I heard you right." Cradling the phone, I pressed my temple. "How much? Because it sounded like you said twenty thousand dollars."

I started to laugh. That couldn't be right. Before I could stop myself, I thought about everything I could do with the money. I could pay off my car. I could quit my day job. I could buy Grandpa and Aunt Helen a lovely dinner. I could even send them on a much-needed, nice trip! And, most importantly, I wouldn't have to make that heinous presentation because I could give my notice! Immediately!

"Yep, you heard me right. Who's laughing in the background?"

I had laughed myself into hyperventilation and had to put my head between my knees. As if through a distant tunnel, I heard Harry calling my name.

"Annie? Annie? Are you still there? Is that you laughing?"

"Oh, uh, yeah. What? Oh, that was someone laughing on T.V. I'm here. This sounds like a great project. What's the next step?"

"I'll email you his name and contact info. Like I said, he does have some anger issues, but you should be okay."

"I feel like there's something you aren't telling me, Harry."

Harry got serious. "Well... Look, Annie, this is a wonderful opportunity for you to prove yourself to us. He actually requested you based on your portfolio with us. Plus, the pay is way above what you normally make. Do you want this gig or not?"

My gut said WAIT! This feels off. But, my pocketbook and work reality won out with their two cents: *Are you crazy? DO IT NOW! It's five times what you normally make as a ghostwriter!* Entry-level ghostwriters don't make that much. Sure, four thousand dollars for a fifty thousand-word book sounds like a lot, but do the math. With a full-time day job and super-weird clients, each book takes about two to three months. And don't forget the taxes.

"Okay, I'll do it."

"Fabulous. I gotta go, but I'll call you tomorrow with more information."

Calming myself with the thought that it would only be for a few months, I pushed down my gut feelings and did a dance around the room. My inner child (who was alarmingly close to the surface) did somersaults and cartwheels. I could finally leave my grey cell!

CHAPTER 2

FTER I HAD A MODEST DINNER of tomato soup and a grilled mozzarella cheese sandwich, I pondered how to word my resignation letter to CritiCentric, and logged onto the laptop they had supplied to me. I really just wanted to ditch the job, but my conscience got the best of me. I didn't want to burn bridges, plus I was grateful to them for giving me the job. Once the machine booted up, I wrote a very short and to-the-point letter. After I wrote it, I went straight to my personal email account and sifted through my messages. I saw Harry's information on the new ghostwriting gig and was satisfied—I hadn't been dreaming. I could really quit my day job. Harry had included the client's contact information and some particulars of this project. After I printed out the files Harry had sent, I arranged them on the coffee table. I looked over his contact information first.

His name, Marcos Landrostassis. I looked at his prison record and criminal complaints. Wow! Whatever the outcome of this book, it had promise of making a mark. From Harry's notes, this guy had been in and out of the prison system multiple times in the last few years.

However, in his notes on the court records, Harry wrote that Marcos claimed he was framed and that the courts were lying. Marcos also claimed that the law enforcement agencies were in collusion with the banks. I supposed anything was possible.

As I read further, I noticed that he had a wife named Diana. No kids.

Harry had made it clear in his email that the spin of this book was to be of an innocent man being wrongly accused. That gnawing feeling in my gut returned as I looked over the documents.

However, necessity made me push that feeling way down. I needed this gig.

I made a few notes for their first interview and decided to call Marcos the next day. Meanwhile, I needed to get ready for my date with a guy named Rick Anderson. I barely knew this guy and wasn't really excited about meeting him for a drink, but I needed to get out there. All of my friends were coupling up, and I was spending way too much time alone.

With my almost black, curly hair, I just let it do its own thing. It would anyway, regardless of what I tried to do anyway. I put on a little makeup. Because I looked so much younger than I was, I tended to keep the makeup minimal. A bit of eyeliner, mascara, and light blush, and I was out the door. I had paired a magenta pink cold shoulder top with a short black skirt, which went well with my dark features and pale skin.

By the time I made it to Smash on Kilbourn, Happy Hour was over, but Rick and I had agreed to meet at eight. I popped onto a barstool and waited. I wasn't familiar with Smash, and the floor plan seemed interesting. I didn't get out much, but I preferred the smaller, cozy drinking establishments that dot Wisconsin's countryside. Smash had blaring music, strobe lights, and—wait!—bird cages. Apparently, they had giant bird cages, which seemed very Mod 1960s era.

Opting for a Moscato while I waited, I demurely sipped my drink and tried to not crane my neck every ten seconds for a sight of Rick. From what I remembered, he had strawberry blond hair and seemed a bit stiff. Yawn! But again—I needed to be more social.

Straightening my skirt, I determined to have a good time tonight.

Hip hop fusion played overhead and I watched the dancers gyrate on the dance floor. Envying how they kept time to the music, I lost myself in the sensations surrounding me.

Time ticked by and before I knew it, I was halfway through my second Moscato at eight-thirty and realizing I had been stood up. Grrr! Frustrating, especially when I hadn't even wanted to do this. The guy had begged me to come out.

Suddenly, I heard her. I heard her before I even saw her. Her cackling, craggly voice reached me from the doorway. Panicked, I looked around for an exit. But she had already sighted her prey and I couldn't leave without being rude.

I felt her sharp talons on my arm and she squealed my name. "ANNIE!"

Oh dear God.

"Hi Tessa. What's up?" I crumpled a little inside.

"Just hanging out! What's up with you? Hey, didn't you have a date tonight?"

How on earth had she known? Michael. He must have mentioned it.

"My plans changed." I said tersely. I shielded myself away from her, but she came around and stuck her face in my mine.

"Awww, poor thing! You were stood up!" At that moment, the entire bar went quiet. Oh, sweet death! Where are you?

I sunk into myself, if that's possible. But how could I deny it? I was clearly dressed up with no place to go, or something like that.

Tessa leaning across the bar, flaunting her goods in her tight, mint green scoop top. She lowered her voice to what she thought was a sexy growl (but sounded a bit scary). "Hey Bartender! What do we have to do to get some shots?"

Her blond platinum hair sat like a cotton candy beacon on her head. And many, skeevy guys came out of the woodwork to do her bidding. Unfortunately, I got the overflow.

While she cackled and held court, I drank the shots handed to me. I normally don't drink much, but people kept buying them. The lights mixed with the music, creating a kaleidoscope of color and sound. The air blurred and people's faces moved in and out of my view. Everything appeared like it was underwater.

"So, Annie, tell me what Karen wanted with you today?" I heard Tessa ask me, but I couldn't see her ruby red lips move.

I felt my lips move, but I'm not sure what I said. My lips formed words like "Karen... books... deadline." I may have laughed a little. Then Tessa laughed more.

People kept whooshing around me. "Oh, she's an innocent-looking one, isn't she?"

"Mmmmm-hmmm, just how I like 'em!"

"I bet she'd be a good dancer!!! Woooohoooo!!!"

And another drink was shoved in my face. A really tall woman with hair and makeup like Dee Snyder offered me her hand. Confused I took it, and got half-dragged to one of the bird cages.

What do they want me to do? Why am I in a bird cage?

I batted hands back that tried to undress me and push my hips into action.

Thoughts swirled in my head. Harry's voice kept repeating, "Hey, doll!" Meanwhile, a vision of Karen handing me those huge books looped.

Suddenly flashes of light went off everywhere. Through

my murky, shot-laden head, I somehow realized that people were taking my picture. I flew out of the bird cage and ran home about three hours before I had to get up.

•••

Despite my aching head, when I woke up, the air smelled crisper. The fall foliage looked more beautiful. The sun shone brighter. For a second, I wondered why I felt so great. I shouldn't feel great. I should feel terrible. No sleep. Far more alcohol for me than normal. Then I remembered: I was giving my notice today. Ah! Life was grand! Bounding out of bed, I made coffee, brushed my teeth, and showered. I changed into one of my best outfits in honor of giving notice. I wore an Ann Taylor dress with a black empire-waist skirt and a peacock blue top. I had been told that the blue in the dress set off my light complexion nicely and helped me look older than fourteen. Sadly, even as a college grad, I still got asked where I went to high school. By high school students. Along with that, I wore my four-inch heels. Take that, Karen and company!

When I got to the building where I worked, I noticed a crowd of ambulances and squad cars in the street. As I got closer, I saw Sally, the receptionist, standing on the sidewalk.

"Hey Sally, what's going on?"

"It's Stan. He had a minor heart attack while he and Karen were going at it on a conference table early this morning."

"Going at what?"

"You know—*it*."

"WHAT? They were doing *it*?"

"You mean, you didn't know? Oh yeah, he and Karen have been at *it* for years. Stan's wife doesn't know a thing. Or at least she didn't. I'm not sure what will happen now." Sally shrugged.

I started to look around but didn't see my boss. "Have

you seen Karen?"

Pulling her cardigan tighter, Sally pointed to one of the squad cars with her chin. "She's over there. She went into shock. The cops told her to just take easy. I think she's going to take a couple of days off."

Crap. There went my two weeks' notice today. Of course, this did mean a reprieve for my presentation. My good mood evaporated and my head began to throb.

"See ya inside, Sally."

"Yeah, see ya." Sally waved absentmindedly as I dragged myself into the building.

I turned on my company-issued laptop. *Beep. Buzz. Gurgle. Has this always sounded so loud?* It snapped to life. *Has this screen always been so bright?* I opened my work email and saw an all-hands meeting notice to explain what had happened to the esteemed (cough, cough) director of CritiCentric, Stan Nickels.

"Annie, did you hear the news?" My coworker Michael poked his head in my cubicle.

"Yeah, I saw the ambulance. Did you know about this?" I asked.

"No. Honest. I had no idea." But his red ears gave him away. "Why are you more pale than usual?"

"Hmmm?" I quirked my brow, wondering how much Michael wasn't sharing. "Oh well, poor Stan. I hope he gets well, regardless of what caused the heart attack. Think he'll have us do a root cause analysis of the reason for it? I'm sorry, I shouldn't joke about it. When's Karen coming back?"

Feeling pretty proud of myself for avoiding his commentary on my appearance, I continued to prepare myself for the day.

"I think I heard—," Michael started. A shrill voice cut him off.

"Hey guys!" Tessa yelled to us. "Yoo-hoo! Whatcha talking about? Me?" Then she proceeded to laugh uproariously as she approached my cubicle.

Michael and I shared a look, and I just barely restrained my eyes from rolling back into my head. Tessa tormented him only slightly less than me.

"See you guys later. I have to go to a meeting." With that, Michael scurried off.

I smirked—I knew he didn't have a meeting scheduled. I snorted as I stifled a laugh.

After he had left, Tessa shooed me further into my cubicle.

"So, guess what?" she said in a stage-whisper.

"What?" I mimicked her stage-whisper.

"Karen put me in charge until she gets back!" Her stage whisper became a shout.

Oh no! my mind screamed. That could not be good, on any level.

Gulping, I played the corporate game and pasted on a big smile. "That's great, Tess. Are we still going to have our staff meeting this afternoon?"

"Yes indeedie!" Tess's voice returned to her creepy stage whisper and she hissed, "Oh, and your presentation is still on for Friday. Don't even think about not doing it."

My face went completely red. I could not find the words I needed. I sputtered a lame, "Wh-what are you talking about?"

Having gotten the desired reaction, Tess left. "Ta-ta, I'm off for now. Have to let the rest of the team know the good news. Hey, could you tell Michael? That's a good girl. Thanks!" She waved her Jungle Red polished nails at me.

How could Karen share confidences with Tessa, a subordinate?! Oh wait! Did I tell her at Smash?

Groan. Last night had become such a blur. I think I did. Holding my head in my hands, I tried to stop the cymbals in my head. Scenes of a giant white feather headdress and six-inch hot pink heels kept replaying in my mind.

Giving notice tasted so much sweeter now. Oh, how I wished I knew more about office politics! I knew nothing of alliances and how to fit in correctly. I had always been taught that a good job spoke for itself.

Humpf. Throughout the day, I could hear Tessa's spiky, crinkly voice asking for Congratulations from everyone she spoke to. Her cackling laugh echoed off the walls, filling every corner of the office floor.

•••

At the designated time, Karen's team, including me, went straight to the regularly scheduled staff meeting. I sat in my usual spot, next to Michael. Eleven people made up the Informatic Systems department, with Karen being the twelfth person. Everyone looked at each other and realized Tessa was missing. Awkward silence ensued. No one wanted to talk about the elephant in the room, a.k.a. "Karen's Misadventure," on company property.

Tick tock. Tick tock. The overhead clock marked time. Fifteen minutes went by as we all stared rather stupidly at each other. We all began to fidget.

Finally, Susan King spoke up, "So, has anyone seen Tessa?"

"I saw her talking to Harvey this morning," said George Jurowski. "Wow, how about that news today?" George tried to play to the audience. No one would even look at him.

"She said she might be a few minutes late," said Tessa's one buddy at the company, Mandy Schuler.

Peeved at being ignored, George said, "If she doesn't get here in five minutes, I'm leaving. I don't care whe—"

"Gimme a T." Tessa's voice boomed from the doorway. Every head snapped to the direction of the sound and mouths dropped open. She wore a red-and-white cheerleader's outfit and had pom-poms. Real pom-poms, not the kind they give to little kids at football games.

She continued to strut on in, doing high kicks,

22

completely oblivious to the pain and confusion on our faces. Even Mandy looked down at her hands. I didn't know where to look. I focused on a tiny dent in the conference room table, willing it to open up and swallow me and everyone else. Being spared the pain of watching this debacle would be lovely. Was that asking too much?

Tessa shouted, "Gimme an E." I glanced up, no such luck. We were all still here. Tessa was making the letter shapes as she shimmied and continued to high kick her way into the conference room.

"Gimme an A. Gimme an M. What are we? TEAM. I can't hear you." She continued to shout. Through the glass walls of the conference rooms, I saw people's heads popping up from their cubicles to see what the ruckus was about. I sank down in my seat a little.

"Team," we all mumbled sheepishly. Michael subconsciously pulled at his collar and studied his hands with far greater interest than they deserved. I saw Susan trying to catch my eye; I avoided her, knowing any kind of smirk or shared laugh would be fatal at this point.

"What?" Tessa shook those pom-poms all around. She strode over to me and yelled, "Annie, I can't hear you!" She shook them in my face.

"Team," I said, slightly louder. I felt my face get as red as a tomato. I slunk down in my seat a little more.

"I still can't HEAR you, Annie! C'mon, Annie. We're all waiting. If you don't yell Team, I'll tell everyone about your little punishment presentation on Friday. Do you even know how to do your job anyway? Better yet, maybe I should tell them about your outing last night!"

My vision started going dim. Everyone's face grew blurry. The harder I tried to focus, the fuzzier everything got.

In my fog, I heard someone say, as if from a distance, "Forget it! I'm not going to say I'm on your stupid team. TEAM! Who the hell wears a cheerleading outfit to work anyway? And pom-poms! Why? Why would you have pom-poms? You look like an idiot! I can't take it anymore! I can't take your phoniness anymore, Tessa!" The voice grew closer. "And I can't take being in a job that I hate! It is too much to ask of anyone! I would rather flip burgers than stay here one minute more! I QUIT!"

As the fog cleared, I realized I had shouted all of this while standing on my chair. A huge crowd had gathered outside of the conference room. And everyone was clapping?

"Annie, are you okay?" Michael gently touched my arm. I looked down at him and blinked a few times. "You look really pale."

I shook my head to clear it more. I realized I'd never felt better. I jumped down from the chair and smiled at everyone in the room. In those 4-inch heels, it's a testament to my adrenaline rush that I didn't break my neck.

Tessa appeared to be shocked into silence. Her mouth formed a perfect O, and steam seemed to be coming from her ears. She narrowed her eyes and looked like she could spit nails.

"I'm A-OK." I strode to the doorway. "Tessa, you treat everyone badly! Eventually, this will come back on you! Don't be surprised when it does! Ta-ta!" I waved to her and almost skipped down the hallway. The applause of my co-workers, er, former coworkers, followed me down the aisle to the door marked Exit.

CHAPTER 3

I LEFT ALL OF MY JUNK IN THE CUBICLE and vowed to never to work in one of those mini-prisons again. For that matter, I never wanted to step foot in that building. I knew that CritiCentric wasn't a bad company, it really wasn't. And I did appreciate that they had given me a job and an opportunity for advancement; however, I learned a lot about myself while I was there. I learned that my temperament and personality were not really suited for having a traditional, nine-to-five job. I liked to work and be useful; so, I wasn't lazy. I identified strongly with Peter from *Office Space* and just preferred to do a different kind of work.

I had very high hopes for this ghostwriting gig, because my Plan B did not exist. In the meantime, I figured CritiCentric could keep my calendar, mug, and anything else I had left behind. The laptop and bag stayed with them anyway.

Once I got home, I changed into sweats and threw my unruly dark curls into a ponytail. To celebrate my little victory (and to avoid dwelling on reality), I put on some music and danced around the living room.

For dinner, I ordered a cheese and pepperoni pizza

from Giovanni's. I added an order of garlic bread for good measure.

I finished a couple of slices and a third of the garlic bread hunk.

I poured myself some diet soda and called my new client, Marcos.

"Hello?" answered a soft, female voice.

"Hi, um, is Marcos available, please?" I pushed down my shyness—I had to make this call. Establishing first contact with clients made me a bit wobbly. I had done it a million times. Every time I told myself that I had nothing to fear. What's the worst the client could do to me anyway?

"No, I'm sorry. He will have to call you back," the voice said rather curtly and with a faint accent. I tried to place the accent. Greek maybe?

"Do you know wh—?"

Click.

I rubbed my temples. Okay. That was weirder than usual. I sat and stared at my phone, willing it to ring.

Imagine my surprise when it did two seconds later. I almost jumped out of skin. Grabbing my phone with shaking hands, I saw Harry's Chicago number.

"Doll."

"Harry?"

"Yeah. Doll. I forgot to tell you something important about this project. Have you called Marcos yet?"

Sigh. My stomach sank a little. I started pacing around my living room.

"Yep. I just tried to call him a few minutes ago. A woman answered the phone. I tried to leave a message, but she hung up on me."

"A woman answered? Hmmm… it must have been his wife, Diana. Well, he's difficult to reach, that's part of what I need to tell you, Sweetheart."

"I'm listening," I ground out through clenched teeth. Whatever joy I had felt from ditching CritiCentric was being replaced by a feeling I knew well—anxiety.

"There's actually a reason why you'll have restricted access to Marcos. He doesn't want visitors."

"Oh, he doesn't like having people over?"

"Kind of."

Harry cleared his throat. "Gosh, I'm starting to feel bad about putting you in this position. I really should have told you how limited your access would be to Marcos."

That struck me as a very odd thing to say. Alarm bells clanged in my head. Suddenly, I realized exactly what Harry was trying to tell me. I reasoned, no, Harry wouldn't do this to me.

I yelled into my phone, "Are you saying he's still in PRISON? What are you doing to me, Harry? Is this why I got this project?"

Flopping onto the couch, I tried to get some perspective. I quit my job for this gig. Oh. My. Gosh. I. Quit. My. Job.

"Ssh. Ssh, Annie! Calm down! No. No, it's not that. He's a little—just a little, mind you—crazy."

"Crazy! Like that makes it better. Well, maybe it does a little. But you said to calm down? Okay, seriously, I'm not even sure I want this project anymore." My mind raced. I could waitress. I like people. I can take food orders. The break from Corporate America will be good.

It had occurred to me that the pay was suspiciously high for this project—something I should have paid more attention to before.

"No, no. Please don't quit this project, Annie! We need you because of your lo—," Harry stopped himself. I burned with curiosity to know what he was about to say. He continued, "What I mean to say is, we really need you to stay with this project. Actually, there's an extra five grand—in advance—if you stay on. I'll bring it up personally, myself. I can meet you up in Door County. Are there any good steak joints up there?"

An extra five thousand? Wait.

"Did you say Door County, Harry?"

He gave a nervous laugh. "Oh yeah, doll, didn't I tell you? I'm gonna need you to temporarily move to Door County for however long this book takes."

"I'm sorry, what?"

"You're going to need to move up there to complete this one."

"Why?"

"He needs to be near his doctor." Then he whispered, "His psychiatrist. He has had some psychotic episodes."

His voice rose again. "Besides, it'll be a nice little vacation for you, right? Anyway, you'll be staying on Brook Harbor. He lives nearby, Turtle Bay, or some similarly crazy named place. I dunno. You live up there, not me."

"I live up there? No, I don't. How close do you think Milwaukee is to Door County?" Squeaking again, I emphatically pointed out, "It really isn't that close! And I thought you'd said I'd have limited access to him. Why do I need to move up there?"

"In addition to vindicating Marcos, the piece is supposed to be a 'slice of life' type of book. He's started a kind of artist colony up in Door County, so you'll need to get a feel for the place."

"The artist colony?"

"No, just the culture of the area. Marcos recommended it."

Anxiety warred with practicality for a few seconds. But, the fact still remained that I had quit my job and had outstanding bills to pay. Plus, it didn't hurt that I loved Door County, and really could use a change. I had grown stagnant in Milwaukee. I felt like my friends were moving on with their lives, while I was still waiting for my adventure.

"Aw, c'mon, Annie. We really need you to do this book."

Practicality and the need for adventure won out. I

ground out, "Fine, I'll do it.

"And you're going to bring up the extra five thousand? Plus, you're going to cover my room and board for the designated time?" I confirmed.

"Yep." Hmmm… he had agreed to that room and board request a little too readily. He must be desperate.

"All right, Harry. This is it, though. No more surprises. Please. I can't take any more surprises. Okay?"

"Yeah sure, Doll. I'll be up Saturday afternoon. We can go over your outline then and I'll give you the bonus check. Oh, and I already stuck the first payment in the mail."

Begrudgingly, I thanked him. "Um, how will I get in touch with Marcos?"

"Let him call you from now on. He has all your contact info. Be ready to answer his call anywhere and anytime. He really doesn't like to be kept waiting."

Oh great!

•••

At ten the next morning, my phone rang, and caller ID said, "Unknown." Tentatively, I answered it.

In for a penny, in for a pound, I thought as I said, "Hello?"

"Hello. Is this Annie Malone?" answered a low, growly voice. He had a very heavy Mediterranean accent. Given his name, I had assumed he came from Greece. Given the growliness of his voice, I didn't dare ask.

"Well, um, yeah, hi. This is Annie. Oh, right, you know that already. I'm going to be writing your book. I'm so glad you call—"

"Of course! Of course! Oh, Harry spoke of you in such glowing terms! You are going to help vindicate me after my terrible ordeal!" Huh, he certainly liked to exclaim things.

"V-vindicate? Well, I don't kn-now about vindication,

29

per se. I d-do know that I'm going to get your story out there." I stammered, "I-I me-mean if you need vindication, then I guess I'm h-here to help."

Mentally, I banged my head against the wall. This guy had me frazzled within 10 seconds of talking to him. How did that happen?

"You must vindicate us! We are pinning all of our hopes on you," continued Marcos. "I have been framed, framed I tell you! And I will have redemption!"

Okay, Sparky, just calm down. I had learned that people got very passionate about their books. They paid a lot of money to Harry and expected their ghostwriter to be a sort of therapist. In my time with Harry, I had heard a lot of bizarre stories and life viewpoints. Typically, I viewed clients with a certain detachment in order to keep my sanity. Marcos seemed to want to pull me into the phone and into his story. Once I realized that, I was able to retain a sense of objectivity (and lose the stammer).

"Marcos, I will do everything I can to get your story told."

"Have you read our case yet? You believe I'm innocent, don't you?" Marcos sounded slightly suspicious.

"Harry sent me some of the files, but he said you could send me additional files. Also, I'd like to set up some time for us to conduct a phone interview."

"The InterGlobal Bank is persecuting me. They are hunting down my family and in cahoots with the police departments. Did you know that? Did you know that the police sent me to prison? Wrongly. They framed me. They said I beat up my tenant and killed her boyfriend. Me, Marcos Landrostassis! I would never do that!" He became agitated again. "I would not do that! I am a proud family man!"

"And I want to help you," I said, amazed at how quickly he could lose focus. I spoke to him slowly and gently, as I would to a toddler. "Let me look through more of the paperwork and let's set up a time to talk Friday." I planned to drive up to Door County Friday morning; I figured I'd be able to interview Marcos once I got up there.

"Yes, yes, of course. We will talk," said Marcos. "Can I call you at three o'clock Friday?"

"Perfect. Thanks for your time." I gave him the rest of my contact information, and he gave me the website where he had stored the files I needed.

"Thank you so much! When you hear my whole story, you will know I am innocent."

With that, he hung up the phone. I shook my head. Where on earth did Harry come up with these people?

CHAPTER 4

WITH HARRY'S ADVANCE, I BOUGHT the most basic laptop possible.

Once I got the laptop home, I had just enough time to prepare for my initial interview with Marcos. I downloaded and read some of the files from Marcos' website. The gaps in his timeline struck me as very odd. Whole pockets of time, years even, were missing from these files. If I had to rely on pure instinct, it felt like the omissions were strategic. The names Tina Delvecchio and Ray Harris kept appearing again and again.

Despite the weird feelings I had about the project, I still found myself temporarily moving up to Door County. My grandfather and Aunt Helen had a special dinner for me with a few of my friends from college and work. We met at Giovanni's for pizza and beer. Since I was leaving so quickly, the party was hastily put together, which suited me just fine. I really didn't relish being the center of attention.

Although the suddenness of my trip shocked many of my friends, they all agreed that I needed a change. I had kind of been spinning my wheels since I had graduated. I hadn't realized it so much as when I ditched my job at

CritiCentric and made my plans to move up to Door County for the fall.

Thus, only two days after walking out of my job, I found myself driving up the interstate to Brook Harbor, Door County. I had found a place to stay, the Lighthouse Inn, and was hoping I could stay there all winter. I wasn't sure how accommodations would work, but I figured with so much unknown at this point, what's one more unknown thing, right?

When I arrived in Door County, I felt a freedom I hadn't known in a long time. It was weird—I was so far from my hometown, but I felt like I had come home for the first time. Fortunately, since it was the middle of October, the leaves had just hit their peak up there. The trees exploded in color and made it hard for me to keep my eyes on the road. Vibrant reds, yellows, and oranges greeted me as I zipped down the road.

As I drove into Brook Harbor, a quaint church and cemetery greeted me. They crested a hill. Driving down the rather steep hill made me feel like I'd end up in Green Bay (the actual bay, not the city). But the road ended right at my destination: The Lighthouse Inn.

If you weren't careful, you could hit the charming little inn. As the road sloped into the quaint village, the inn's property jutted into the intersection. Oh, and if you missed that, there was a big picture of a sea captain with the "Lighthouse Inn" sign on the side of the building. I figured out where to park and went to the reservation desk. At least I thought it was the reservation desk. After ten minutes of waiting, I thought that maybe I should try the adjacent room, which looked like the bar. Grabbing my stuff, I trudged over to the bar.

By that point, all I wanted was a big, juicy burger and a cold beer. I was in luck. The Lighthouse also boasted a microbrewery on its premises.

As I approached the bar, out of the corner of my eye, I saw a pile of boxes moving towards me. The boxes looked like they could topple over any minute. I couldn't tell whether they were full or empty.

"Out of my way! Out of my way!" said the boxes.

I turned towards the unseen voice. "Hey! Do you need some help?"

"Sure, can you grab the top box?"

"I think so," I said, as I stood on my tiptoes to reach the box. As I grabbed it, a smiling face framed by curly blonde hair beamed down at me. The bartender was a taller-than-average woman, about my age, with long, curly blonde hair held back with a headband.

"Thanks! I think I grabbed more than I realized!" The smiling face laughed. After putting the rest of her load down on the bar and gesturing for me to do the same, she put out her hand. "Hi! I'm Lizzy Holloway. Are you staying here?"

We shook hands. "My name is Annie Malone and, yes, I'm staying here. And I need to talk to someone about extended rates?"

"Oh sure, no problem. Kitty's the owner and she can help you with that, but she's out right now."

She said that last bit over her shoulder. After rummaging around in the cupboards under the cash register, she came back with a binder.

"Yep, I see you right here. Okay, you're in Room 4. Here's your key. Yeah, I know, we're an inn—we have old-fashioned keys here." She scrunched up her face.

"Oh, and Annie, I almost forgot, you get a couple of coupons for your stay here. You get a free sampler platter of our micro-brewed beers and a free drink anytime." She put her hand to the side of her mouth, and stage whispered, "But come right back down and I'll give you another free drink for helping me out."

"In that case, I'll be right back down," I said. "I'm famished! I just realized I forgot to eat breakfast in my excitement to get up here."

With my free hand, I grabbed the coupons, thanked her

again, and negotiated my gear up the narrow staircase to my room. Housed in an old Cape Cod-type dwelling, the inn had eight rooms. I'm not sure whether it was an attempt at "old-world charm" or cost issues, but the place had a sense of being a bit rundown. The seeming fragility of the building lent credence to the rumors of the place being haunted. Supposedly, famous gangster Al Capone's stepson haunted the roof and attic.

Once I put my stuff in the room and washed up, I grabbed my purse, ambled back down to the bar, and settled in. It felt good to be sitting still. For the past couple of days, I felt like I had been moving nonstop.

"Do you need a drink?" Without waiting for my answer, she went behind the bar, opened a bottle, and started pouring. Done pouring, she thrust the heady brew at me. "Here, I owe you. The first one is on me, and I think you'll really like this beer. If you don't, I'll get you something else. Thanks again for helping me out!" She walked away to help the only other patron at the bar, a guy who looked like he had been sitting there for ages.

Taking a deep breath, I let out a huge sigh and took a long drink from the beer.

"Wow!" Everyone else in the bar turned to look at me, the strange girl with the excessively loud exclamation. (Fortunately, there were only three other people there—Lizzy, the other bar patron, and one of the kitchen guys getting a soda.) I turned bright red and sheepishly said, "Sorry. That's just really good." The Lighthouse had taken advantage of Door County's cherry orchards and created a wonderful beer.

Completely embarrassed, I fumbled around in my purse. I had resolved to bury my embarrassment in a book while I ate lunch.

"Whatcha reading?" Lizzy popped over just as I pulled out the book.

"A mystery."

"Who's it by?"

"Susan Boyer."

"Oh, she's such a fun read!"

"She is, isn't she?" Warming to the topic, I began to lose my shyness.

"Oh, definitely! Glad you like that beer. It's my favorite, too. Guys don't usually like it, so they tend to leave more for us." Lizzy winked. She wiped the bar in front of me, then laid down a menu. "You had mentioned you'd want lunch. Just let me know when you're ready to order." With that, Lizzy went off to unpack boxes.

I found what I wanted immediately—a big hamburger and artery-clogging French fries. Yum. Once I gave the universal sign that I was ready (putting the closed menu back on the bar), Lizzy stopped by and took my order. After dropping off my order, she stopped back to check on my drink and ask me how it was going.

I told her and somehow or other, we got on the topic of how I ended up in Brook Harbor. I gave her the complete scoop on my new ghostwriting gig and how I had quit my job in Milwaukee.

By the time I had finished, my food was ready. Lizzy went back to the kitchen to get it. When she came back, she was still shaking her head over how I quit my job.

"Wow!" Lizzy stared at me, open-mouthed. "Did you really walk out of a meeting like that?"

"Yup."

"That's what most people dream of doing and you did it!" she said with seeming admiration. "You have guts." She nodded for emphasis.

"Guts. Stupidity. It's a very fine line, and right now I think I'm a little on the stupid side."

"Oh, don't be so modest. Honestly, I think this book sounds great! It sounds like just the project you needed! Why aren't you more excited?"

I shared my apprehension regarding Marcos Landrostassis and his criminal record.

"He expects this book to vindicate his family." I

punctuated my words by stabbing my coleslaw with a fork. "And Harry is really putting a lot of pressure on me. Subtly, you know what I mean?"

"Yep. He's putting out his neck for this guy, for whatever reason. Therefore, you are on the hook to turn out a good product. Hmm... Landrostassis... why does that name sound familiar?"

"I know, I was thinking the same thing. The name sounds so familiar, but I just can't place it. Maybe it's just one of those names." I gnawed thoughtfully on a fry. "I know what you mean about producing a good book, though. And, despite giving me some of the weirdest projects ever, Harry has treated me pretty well. No, there's something else intangible here. Something feels off. You have no idea. This guy is a whacko. I'm not sure if he's a narcissist or has multiple personalities. Or has a combination of that. I suppose it's a good thing he lives close to his psychiatrist—he certainly needs one."

"You'll be okay. Just write this book. Make a name for yourself in publishing circles, then you can be a little choosier. Also, then we can read your book for our book club!"

"Yeah, you're right. This isn't like my first ghostwriting book." At least I could laugh about it now.

"What was it about?"

"This woman thought dolphins were aliens from another planet. She also thought they were key to our victory in the Revolutionary War."

"I think we did read that for book club. You wrote that?" Lizzy threw back her head and laughed. I joined her. We laughed until our sides hurt and made tentative plans to have lunch together the next day. Lizzy promised to show me some of the sights and sounds of Turtle Bay, a town north of Brook Harbor.

"And here is one of the members of our book club! Hey, Janie, come here a sec!" I waited while a stylish woman in her mid-thirties made her way over to us. With her sleek, dark bob, she looked chic, but not snobby.

"Hey, Lizzy! Who do we have here?"

"Janie, this is Annie Malone, she's going to be staying here for a while. And, Annie, this is Janie Nicholson. She is Kitty's sister and co-owner of the Lighthouse."

We exchanged pleasantries and shook hands.

"Where is she anyway?"

"I thought she was with you, actually."

"Can you let her know I stopped by?"

"Of course! Oh, and Janie, get this… do you remember that book we read with the dolphins and robots?"

Janie laughed in recollection, "Yes, that was one crazy book."

I turned bright red. Lizzy gestured towards me, "Meet the author!"

"You wrote that? But wait, wasn't it written by an older woman from another culture? Like, it was her autobiography or something, if I remember correctly."

"Yeah, about that. I was just telling Lizzy here about my ghostwriting project. And I happened to write that book."

"What book?"

"The one you were just talking about."

Janie looked perplexed, "But wasn't that an autobiography?"

I cleared my throat uncomfortably. Why did I feel uncomfortable? I wasn't the lady who claimed it was my autobiography.

When I didn't answer, Lizzy interjected, "So, do you mean to tell us that most autobiographies are written by people like you? Ghostwriters?"

"Yep," and with that, I smiled, waved, and headed upstairs to my room.

•••

According to rumors, my room was the most haunted,

and I wondered if I'd have any ghostly visitors.

Not only was there the possibility of meeting the ghost of Al Capone's stepson, but I had read online that a lady in white often appeared on the staircase. Why is it always a lady in white anyway? Apparently, the lady in white had died in the late 1880s after she heard her fiancé's boat had sunk in Lake Michigan. In any case, I wasn't sure whether or not I hoped to see a ghost.

In preparation for the interview, I changed into sweats and got the prerequisite tools: a can of diet soda, pen, and pad of paper. I regretted not having a phone-recording device. I resolved to get one and hook it up to my cell phone before this project ended. At the very least, I should've gotten headphones with a microphone. Resignedly, I opted to put Marcos on speakerphone— much easier for taking notes. Of course, getting to meet in person is preferred over all.

I paced my room. At three on the dot, my phone rang. *Breathe, breathe, I told myself. I answered the phone.*

"Hello? This is Annie," I said, slightly out of breath.

"Hey, hey, Annie. Why didn't you call me today?" demanded Marcos. "I waited for you to call."

"You did? Because I thought we had arranged for you to call me. I thought you preferred it that way." *You wanted that, since you are a control freak with extreme trust issues*, I silently added.

"What do you mean, what I prefer? How do you know what I prefer? Do you think I prefer being persecuted by everyone?" He sounded a little angry. And a lot crazy.

"Um, yeah. I mean, no, not at all." I hoped not all of our conversations would be so circular and fuzzy. In the corner on my mind, a huge, gonging warning bell went off, but I plowed through and ignored it. Since I had so gloriously and irreversibly quit my day job, I had to keep this project.

"Okay, well, I don't know what to tell you then. I guess we'll just have to talk now."

Now? Inwardly, I wondered when else he was planning to talk. We had supposedly arranged to talk now. Was he all there?

Outwardly, I said, "Sure, of course." Settling onto a chair, I held the pen poised.

"What do you want to know?" he asked, amiably. Okay, seriously, I felt so confused now. First he was all angry; now he was all nicey-nice. I really needed to get used to these mood shifts. He seemed to go from disgruntled to gruntled, and back again, in seconds.

Gathering my courage, I asked Marcos if we could meet in person soon. I pointed out, quite reasonably, that I had moved up to Door County to work on this book.

With this request, I encountered a mini-, and not altogether unexpected, explosion. My mercurial client emphatically stated, "No! We will not meet until I say we can meet. And I am not ready for us to meet!" Well, that wasn't as bad as I thought it would be.

"Oh, okay. Sure, no problem. Why don't we start with your issues with the bank? After you sued them, it seems to be when all of your troubles started."

"Good thinking. My wife and I had a great relationship with the InterGlobal Bank for many years. We enjoyed the bank's services as customers and borrowers. This bank had enabled us to get a loan for a $350,000 condo up here, while I worked a seasonal forestry job and my wife worked as a cashier at a clothing store. We planned to use that rental property to better ourselves. Sadly, everything changed when the InterGlobal bank severely screwed up one of our loans. They raised our monthly payment by forty percent. Our mortgage payment had been $1500, but now it was $2100."

"Wow, that's a huge jump." I wondered how people in forestry and retail could afford a $350,000 condo duplex, but figured he would get to that.

"It was. We weren't prepared for it and we sued the bank to get them to fix the error. We needed to get their attention."

"I'm sure you did get it," I said.

"Get what?"

"Their attention." Oh my goodness, I wondered what I had gotten myself into. I felt like I had fallen into the "Who's on First?" routine.

"Are you gonna let me tell the story?"

In a small voice, I said, "Sure, go ahead."

"Anyway, the bank seemed to have bought our attorneys. And, the cops started harassing us. After we won the suit against InterGlobal bank, my downstairs tenant got into a huge fight with her boyfriend. This tenant, Tina Delvecchio, drank like a fish. When she drank, she became loud and had combative arguments. On this particular occasion, she started screaming at and threatening her boyfriend, Ray Harris. They became extremely disruptive. They actually broke my window!"

"Wait, let me get this straight. Were they in your apartment or Tina's?"

"Tina's. When I say 'mine,' I mean mine as the landlord. Are you gonna let me finish?" Not surprisingly, Marcos did not wait for an answer. "Anyway, they smashed the window to pieces. Most of the glass landed outside. Since I had heard everything, I went outside to start cleaning up the mess. Suddenly, the cops showed up and started accusing me of beating Tina. And they accused me of doing damage to my own property. What, am I crazy?"

I withheld comment at this time.

He continued, "Naturally, I denied the allegations and stated that I was just cleaning up the mess. I told them the fight was between Ms. Delvecchio and her boyfriend. I told them to ask the witnesses. I went back inside my apartment. I figured that would be the end of it."

I waited a few beats before asking, "But it wasn't?" I dared not breathe lest he get on me for interrupting again.

"No, it wasn't. Not by a long shot. The cops came back

to my apartment and beat me up in front of my wife! They said that I had issued a death threat for Tina! I kept telling them to 'ask the witnesses.' A few weeks went by, and Tina got into another fight with Ray. This time, she stabbed the guy."

"She stabbed the guy? Really?" I shook my head. Truth really could be stranger than fiction. I imagined Tina with a black, pink-tipped Mohawk haircut and sharp features, holding out a jackknife.

"Believe it! What the hell! Will you let me finish already? Do you interrupt all of your clients this much? Anyway, after Ray was stabbed, they blamed me. They roughed me up again and hauled me down to the station. But Tina came forward and admitted what she had done. As soon as they found out Tina had done it, they let her go. They didn't even charge her. Nothing. They reasoned that she was an admitted alcoholic, and it was a crime of passion. Yet they had no problem coming after me with no evidence and no witness. During the first incident, she never brought charges against me and never told the police I threatened her in any way. In every incident, it's always the cops saying I beat someone up or I threatened someone. It's all lies. Everything's a fabrication.

"Eventually, I made the connection between the banks and the cops because that bank handles the cops' main pension fund. These guys all stick together, thick as thieves. After we won the lawsuits, not only did we suffer at the hands of the cops, but they would not allow us, the Landrostassis family, to bank with them. They refused to let us pay our mortgages. They wanted to intentionally send us into financial ruin. They would go as far as calling the police to remove me and Diana from the bank."

"Wait! Who's Diana again?" I felt I had read that name somewhere, but Marcos was throwing so much information at me.

"My wife! Now, stop interrupting. Where was I? Oh yes, they prevented us from making payments on the rental property and the bank was allowed to get control of the rentals and two of the other buildings we had previously bought! And they sent me to prison! For crimes I didn't even commit!"

Writing furiously, I was determined to get all of his narrative down on a paper. If what Marcos said was true, it sounded like he and Diana had gotten a raw deal. He had said "the Landrostassis family" like I was supposed to know who they are. I knew I had heard the name before this project. Lizzy had mentioned that the name sounded familiar to her too.

"Hey, would it be okay with you if I talked to this Tina Delvecchio? I'm wondering if she can give me any insight as to her thoughts on why you and your family have been so harassed." It seemed like a logical step to me. I figured I could have a quick phone conversation with Tina Delvecchio and get my impressions. Drunk or not, Tina had to have some interesting insight into this whole story. I reasoned that Marcos' problem wasn't really with Tina anyway; it was with the police who had roughed him up.

"You don't need to interview her. Why would you need to interview her? What would she tell you that I'm not already telling you?" Marcos demanded.

He was getting really agitated. "Tell me, WHAT WOULD SHE TELL YOU THAT I'M NOT ALREADY TELLING YOU?"

Okay, now he was yelling. I started to get a stomachache while my stupid client yelled in my ear. Very uncool. I resolved to talk to Harry about this one. A slap would feel better than this verbal onslaught. My stomachache grew worse the more he talked.

"Why are you yelling at me? I'm just trying to help, you big goon."

Oh my gosh, I realized I had just called my volatile client a goon. Uh oh.

"Did you just call me a goon?"

"I'm sorry, what? Our connection is bad. I can't hear

you. Someone is knocking on my door." I felt like such a wimp. Now, where had my courage run off to?

"Look, if you don't want to do this book the way I'm paying you to do it, just say so. I can call Harry and he can find someone else."

My stomachache kicked into high gear. Which was worse: poverty or dealing with this schlub? Fear of living on the streets won out.

"No, no... you are exactly right, Marcos. I do apologize. It's been a long day, what with the drive up here and getting situ—," I said, trying to smooth his ruffled feathers.

Now it was his turn to interrupt me. "I can't talk to you anymore today." He still sounded extremely upset. "Let me think about how to continue with this. I'll be in touch with you tomorrow with my decision."

"Marcos, seriously. I didn't mean anything by it." He had already hung up.

Crap!

CHAPTER 5

CAUGHT UP IN THE RECENT EVENTS, I daydreamed about how quickly life can change as I drove down the highway to a grocery store in Michigan City. I figured since Harry was still paying for it, I should get some good snacks for my room at the inn while I could. Plus, I needed some Milk of Magnesia for the stomachache Marcos gave me. Between my digestive issues and being super distracted, I totally missed the car braking in front of me. Until I was about one foot away from it. As my heart flew to my throat, I simultaneously prayed and slammed on the brakes. I only started breathing again when I didn't hear the crunch of metal. I heard what sounded more like an aggressive scraping. I slapped my forehead. Darn it all! Not another accident! Granted, this seemed like just a fender-bender, but still...

I resigned myself to the inevitable as I opened the car door to exchange insurance information. As I pushed open the door, I encountered resistance and felt a thud. Then, I heard a howl of pain and a muffled, "Ah you tayin' to kiw me?"

Startled, I leapt out of the car and looked down to see a man. In great pain. Writhing on the ground and holding his nose.

Immediately, I bent down over him. "Are you okay?" Oh dear! Oh dear! This isn't good! That made two accidents in as many months. Just last month, I had t-boned a deputy sheriff's car. And the year before, I had totaled my car when it slid under a semi. Had I not ducked? Shudder.

"Wha ah you doig? Why did you opah ya dooh? I thing you brog mah noze! Aargh!"

I decided that the best defense is a strong offense. "Well, what do you think you were doing, sneaking up to my door! I was just about to get out of the car and assess the damage! Obviously, I didn't see you there! Do you think if I had seen you there, I would have opened the door like that? Do you? Do you?"

By the time I had finished my tirade, he was vertical and staring at me as though I'd grown a second head.

The first thing I noticed about him was the gash across his nose and the profuse bleeding. The next thing I noticed was the scowl his mouth made. The last thing I noticed was that his piercing eyes made me feel flush. Mentally, I admonished myself. A cute guy finally crosses my path and what do I do? Crash into his car and break his nose. Well, possibly break his nose. I wasn't a doctor and couldn't make a diagnosis. However, his nose was really bleeding a lot.

He kept glaring at me as he held his nose together. Silently, he handed me a business card and turned on his heel. Speechless, I stared after him.

In stunned silence, I watched him drive away. I looked down at the card in my hand, which read:

DONOVAN ARCHER
Insurance Agent
920-555-0301

"Great! What do I do now?" I thought. I never got to give him my insurance information. I shrugged and pocketed his card. The mysterious exchange suited me just fine actually. I didn't relish having this added to my already abysmal traffic record. Since he left, I skulked away, hoping to keep this little crash quiet.

•••

That night and next morning went so slowly, I thought I would go barking mad. I hated waiting for anything. This time, I felt like I was waiting for my future to be decided by a nut job. Harry called in the morning to give his estimated time of arrival for Saturday night and asked me to make his reservations at the Lighthouse Inn. While waiting to meet Lizzy for lunch, I decided to put my time to good purpose and wrote the outline and the first 2,000 words for the book. I figured if I had work to show for it, I could use that as an argument to keep the project. In addition, I went online and researched some information about the InterGlobal bank and additional mortgage terminology. The weird thing was, the more I learned about the way mortgages work, the more confused I became about Marcos' situation. What confused me even more was why he had yelled at me. My questions hadn't really been that probing. Clearly, I had struck a nerve with him, and I wasn't even sure how it had happened.

Fortunately, I had a lunch date with my new friend, Lizzy, to take my mind off things. Since Lizzy lived Turtle Bay with her sister's family, we had arranged to meet up there at Janie's shop, then go to lunch.

•••

Feeling somewhat better, I found Janie's boutique fairly easily and parked a few doors down from it. Usually notoriously late, I managed to get there before Lizzy to look around.

Janie Nicholson, Kitty Breckenridge's sister and silent

co-proprietor of the Lighthouse Inn, had bought space in a renovated old mill for her pet project, this boutique. Lizzy had given me a little of Janie's backstory when we arranged to meet in Turtle Bay. After Janie's divorce, she had moved back home to Door County. Right about the same time, Kitty was looking for a partner for her inn, and Janie was looking for way to invest her recent divorce settlement. Since the sisters were close enough to enjoy each other's company, and mature enough to respect each other's boundaries, the partnership worked really well.

The exposed Cream City brick allowed the beautiful clothes to "pop" perfectly. For decoration, Janie had hung up select pieces from that season's collection to entice shoppers. I eyed a gorgeous ruffled sweater... then remembered that at five feet nothing and 100 pounds even, ruffles made me look like a 10-year-old.

As I made my way to the back of the shop, Janie peeked out from behind a mannequin she was dressing. "Hey Annie! Good to see you up here. Are you meeting Lizzy? Take a look around," she said as she draped a gorgeous blue knit over her arm. "Try out some cookies and cider." She pointed to a small table laden with treats and placed next to two overstuffed, yellow chairs next to the big front window.

"Hi Janie! Cookies and cider? As if this place could get more charming! Yeah, we're supposed to have lunch at that Irish pub down the street."

"Dublin's?"

"Yup."

"Be sure to try their salmon sandwich. It is to die for."

"I really love your shop! How's business after the tourist season ends?"

"Not too bad. I'm really hoping that things pick up after Halloween. But it isn't bad at all!" Janie smiled as she spoke.

"Hey guys!"

Janie and I turned towards the door as Lizzy came in.

Before I could say a word, Lizzy saw Janie's plate of cookies. "Cookies! Oh great! I'm famished. Do you care if I have one or two or ten?"

Janie smiled. "Sure, no problem. I have more in the back. Well, I'll let you two look around. I need to get back to dressing her." Janie gestured towards the half-dressed mannequin.

Lizzy dragged me over to the sweaters and pulled one from the pile.

"What do you think of this one?"

I gasped, "Oh my gosh! That's my color! Where did you find this?"

Lizzy gestured around the shop.

Nudging Lizzy, I laughed and said, "you know what I mean!"

"Yeah, I thought you might like it. I came here the other day and saw this. When we met, I immediately remembered this sweater, which is one of the reasons I suggested we meet here." Next, Lizzy held up a lime green sweater with bright orange piping. We both shuddered at the color combination.

"And you have to get it!" insisted Lizzy.

"The green and orange sweater?" I said in mock horror.

Lizzy laughed, "Yeah, not the blue one that's clearly perfect for you."

I held up the peacock blue sweater and pirouetted in front of the mirror. "I do think you're right—it's meant to be! I think half of my wardrobe is this color—I love it!"

Lizzy added, "Seriously, if you don't get it, it will be a sin and you will have to go to confession."

"I think you should get it. The blue complements your coloring," said a surprisingly male voice behind me. I whirled around and gasped.

My jaw dropped as I recognized the face belonging to that voice. Feeling a blush coming on, I sputtered, "Hey! You're the—." His smile stunned me into silence. I promptly stopped talking and turned bright red. Flustered, I turned out to grab Lizzy, only to see Lizzy and Janie giggling by the cash register.

"Yeah, and you're the chick who hit me," Donovan said, smiling even bigger. "Your dimples are cute when I'm not writhing in pain."

"Of all the arrogant…"

"Arrogant what?"

"Arrogant yous!" I stomped my foot in frustration.

"You walked away without even saying a word yesterday. I had no idea if you were okay!"

"Well, as you can see…" He grinned broadly and made a sweeping gesture from his head to his shoes.

Now that he stood before me without blood squirting out of his nose, I got a good look at him. He wore a black leather jacket and perfectly fitted blue jeans. I realized that his dark hair and piercing eyes offset his bandaged nose, and he simply smoldered.

"Are you serious?" I squinted up at him. "First you-."

Before I could get really started, Lizzy ran up and grabbed my arm, "Okay, Annie Oakley, let's get you outta here. Janie, can you please put the sweater on hold? Thanks!"

Lizzy and I heard Janie's "No problem!" as Lizzy dragged me to the restaurant next door.

On the sidewalk outside Dublin's Irish Pub, Lizzy let go of me. I turned to face her, expecting her to be appalled. All she said was, "My, you are a feisty one, aren't you?"

That is when I guessed I had made a friend for life.

I had the grace to look penitent for my outburst. I hung my head a little, "Yeah, I've had a busy couple of days. What with this project, moving up here, and, uh, hitting that guy with my car door."

"Oh! Do tell! So you know that guy?"

"If breaking someone's nose counts for knowing someone, then yeah."

Lizzy cocked her eyebrow. "A broken nose is included in this story? Oh, this is going to be good!"

We promptly went into Dublin's and got seated immediately.

CHAPTER 6

LIZZY AND I ORDERED OUR FOOD and drinks. I took Janie's advice and got the salmon sandwich. Lizzy opted for the Shepherd's pie.

"Okay, give. You realize you kind of made quite a scene, right?"

"Good thing it was just you and Janie in there, then, isn't it?"

While we waited for our food, I filled Lizzy in on how I got into a little fender-bender. I also shared that I slammed my car door in Donovan Archer's face. In context, she said she understood the exchange a little better now. We had just gotten our food when Janie came into the restaurant.

"Sorry to interrupt, but I got a chance to take lunch and thought I'd crash your party. Is that okay?" Janie asked.

"Sure! The more the merrier!"

"Of course!"

While I devoured my salmon sandwich, Lizzy filled Janie in on the highs and lows from my interviews with Marcos. They took a brief break for Janie to order her own salmon sandwich for lunch. Once Lizzy finished telling

Janie about Marcos, Janie wasn't sure what to make of him either.

"I feel for ya, Annie. That's a tough one," Janie commiserated with me.

"At least the woman who wrote the book for Liberace was consistently nice. Crazy, but nice," I bemoaned.

Janie started at my mention of Liberace. She looked at us questioningly.

"Yeah, consistency really makes a difference," Lizzy agreed.

"She certainly wasn't normal, but she never raised her voice. However, I'll just have to man up and deal with it. Harry is driving up tonight and I'll tell him what's going on then." As an aside to Janie, I explained how she wrote the book with Liberace as her audience.

"Dedicated to him?"

"No, no, he was her actual intended audience."

"Wow. So, who's Harry? How does he figure into it?" asked Janie.

Lizzy interjected, "He's Annie's Big-time Editor. Go on, Annie, tell Janie what you told me about him." She took the last bite of her Shepherd's pie.

"Eh. He seems okay, but I'm not sure how vested he is in this project. I have a feeling like this is a personal favor for someone. He gave me a huge bonus after I almost bailed on the project. He's supposed to be bringing it tonight."

Once Janie had her food, we switched over to more fun topics. They filled me in on some of the colorful characters in the area. Lizzy and Janie seemed to know everyone from Brook Harbor to Roses Rock, the southernmost and northernmost towns on Door County's west coast, respectively. I filed this useful information away for later.

They explained that Door County's name was also called "Death's Door County."

"Isn't that a little dark?"

"Well, that's probably why it's been shortened," explained Janie. "I mean, I suppose people would still be attracted a macabre name like that, but Door County just sounds lighter."

"Why was it called that anyway?"

"Because of the dangerous strait between Washington Island and Roses Rock. Back in the day, a lot of shipwrecks happened there."

"Hence, the large number of lighthouses up here. That makes sense. What's Roses Rock like?"

Janie laughed a little, "Oh, that's all the way on the northern tip of the peninsula. We don't go there."

"Don't let Janie fool you, Annie," Lizzy smiled. "She's just having fun with you. The peninsula isn't that big. Roses Rock is only 20 minutes away. I'd be happy to show you around there sometime next week."

"Thanks. I'd love that."

After we all finished lunch, we parted ways. Of course, I was still nervous about my upcoming call from Marcos, but the lunch definitely helped take my mind off it. I was relieved that Janie hadn't asked about Donovan and my abrupt exit; I gave her a lot of credit for being discreet.

•••

Back at the inn, I continued writing until I got ready to meet my boss face-to-face. We had decided that we would meet in the inn's restaurant.

Until about four o'clock, I continued working on a book that might never see the light of day.

I really didn't think I'd ever hear from Marcos again. He had been so unstable and illogical. Imagine my shock when he called about two hours before Harry was due to arrive. When the phone rang, I thought it was Harry and picked it up without even looking at the Caller ID.

"Hello, Annie! How's my favorite ghostwriter doing?" Marcos cheerfully asked when I answered the phone.

"Um, fine. Great. How are you?" He sounded really happy. Was Marcos giving a class on 101 ways to confuse your ghostwriter? Because he was succeeding mightily.

"Very well, thank you. Okay, let's get to work. Where did we leave off yesterday?" *Um, you wanted to fire me from the project and have Harry assign a new writer*, I thought.

"Sure. Great. Yeah, let's get to work," I muttered. "I didn't write out any questions for today. I just thought we'd continue with your narrative. If that's okay with you?" Nerves made my voice raise more than usual at the end of the question. He seemed to like hearing the sound of his voice, and it took the onus of communication off me. Win-win.

So, he proceeded to repeat EVERYTHING he had shared yesterday.

Since I didn't need to pay attention or take notes, I completely stopped listening to him. He went on unfettered for about 40 minutes. Suddenly, I realized, he was talking about something different.

"...and I was out walking with my wife. When I stopped to talk to a different neighbor, I walked away from my wife for a few seconds. Literally, in the blink of an eye, the dog lunged at Diana. She was only trying to pet him, and that damn dog scratched her. I know that dog would have done further damage but in the nick of time, I was able to reach Diana. With one hand, I pulled the dog off of her in order to prevent any further injuries. Feeling that the dog might cause more injury to others if it continued to run wild, I took the dog and put it in my car. I intended to take the dog to the dog pound."

Hesitantly, I asked, "What kind of a dog?"

He ignored my question completely and kept going. Reasoning it was probably for the best, I kept quiet.

"My neighbor saw me from her front door. She screamed for me to let the dog go and that she'd already called the cops on me. Sure enough, I heard squad cars in the distance. One of the cops got me with his stun gun."

A stun gun? Wow, I didn't know anyone who'd been zapped with a stun gun before.

"When I came to, I was on my way to the police station again. I didn't know what had happened to my wife. Let me tell you, this was police brutality and torture at its finest. I screamed at the cops, 'Where is my wife? What have you done with her?' They just looked at me oddly and asked if I wanted to be stunned again. Once they got to the station, they booked me and jailed me. When my friend paid the bail, he told me that my wife was okay."

"Did the whole thing come to trial?"

"It did. I asked my other neighbors if I could have them tell my lawyer about the dog incident and the danger her animal posed. I wanted to tape record their conversations with my attorney, Jim Donaldson. They knew the kind of people we were, and they said yes. While I listened to these conversations on the other line, I couldn't believe what my ears were hearing. My lawyer. The lawyer who I was PAYING. This man betrayed me. He was defending the police, saying that this incident probably happened because I had a Doberman pinscher, and the Westie could smell the dog on my wife."

Oh my gosh, all this fuss over a West Highland terrier? They were like little toys. He claimed that a Westie brutally attacked an adult? I wasn't even sure that was physically possible. You could put them in your pocket. *Focus, Annie, focus!* I told myself.

"Soon after that incident, I had gone to the coffee shop. As I went back to my car, a cop confronted me and asked if I could produce any ownership papers for the car. I couldn't. He told me the car had been reported as stolen. His partner came out of nowhere and knocked me in the head with his flashlight. Again, they dragged me into jail. This time, they brought me up on charges of Grand Theft Auto. They were accusing me stealing MY OWN CAR! Needless to say, I was outraged!"

"What did you do?"

"What could we do? I was becoming afraid for my life. To make matters worse, my lawyer, Jim Donaldson, seemed to be in on the setup. He tried to convince me to stop recording my conversations with him. He told me that through these recordings, the police were claiming I had gone off the deep-end, and that the recordings actually would hurt me in court."

"And the court case did happen, right?"

"Yes, while the two other cases were pending, they sent me to prison on other trumped-up charges."

And then I asked the magical question. When in doubt of any kind, always ask this question: Why?

I phrased it thusly: "Why do you think all of this is happening to you and your family?" I did not expect what happened next. Especially when he had sounded so cheerful at the beginning of the interview.

"Are you in on this? Who sent you?" he hissed into the phone. "Unless you tell me who is putting you up to these questions, I will find you." A shiver went up my spine.

With that, he hung up the phone. I sat in stunned silence for a few minutes, wondering what to do. *What I gotten myself into?*

CHAPTER 7

I TRIED TO CALL HARRY ON HIS cell phone. No answer. I didn't want to leave a message. What would I even say at this point? Besides, Harry was already on his way. Since talking to Lizzy and Janie, I had a growing suspicion Harry knew way more about Marcos and this project than he had shared with me. I wondered what was really going on and how deeply Harry was involved. I also wondered if Marcos was completely sane. He seemed a little insane to me. I had relatives who were a little insane, and Marcos trumped their behavior in spades. Deep breaths. I looked at the clock and was shocked back into reality. I had only 20 minutes to get ready before I needed to meet Harry downstairs. As I hopped in the shower, I could hear thunder and lightning outside. Great, atmosphere. Just what I needed.

By the time I got out of the shower and dressed, the storm raged full blast. Lightning electrified the sky outside the window. I dressed in my jade sweater and a pair of black pants and beat the buzzer by ten minutes. As I tousled my curls, and put on make-up, someone knocked on the door. I jumped about 10 feet. The storm and situation with Marcos had made me edgier than I realized.

When I had opened the door, I fully expected to see an inn employee. Instead, a man, who I could only assume was Harry, stood there, and I was pleasantly surprised to see that my mental image matched what he really looked like. That almost never happened. Yet, before me stood an Elliot Gould lookalike, and the first words out of his mouth were, "Hey, doll! Good to see you!"

"Great to meet you face-to-face, Harry." We shook hands and he came in.

He said he didn't want to wait downstairs since he had brought a little gift basket for me. I was touched by the gesture even though I knew it was a marketing thing. The gift basket included a white mug with the name of his vanity publishing company emblazoned in black on the side, a sticky notes pad, keychain, and a couple of pens. Regardless of the marketingness of it all, a gift is a gift and I smiled as I thanked him.

We made our way down to the Lighthouse Inn's bar-slash-restaurant. Harry got his room key and arranged for his suitcase to be taken to his room while we waited for them to clear a table for us. Briefly, I made eye contact with Lizzy, who was tending bar. She mouthed, "Is that Harry?" I discreetly nodded. Once Harry had his room reserved, we were shown our table.

During dinner, I brought Harry up-to-date on the happenings with Marcos. Harry just shook his head. Clearly, he had dealt with these shenanigans from Marcos in the past, which made Harry's next words so surprising. I had expected an understanding ear. I did not expect Harry's actual reaction.

"Crap, Annie. What did you do to set him off? You are here to do a job. Now do it!"

Puzzled, I looked around at the other patrons. People were starting to stare at us. "Um, Harry, can you please keep it down a little? Why are you so upset with me?"

"You are gonna blow it! You seem determined to make me, and the company I've built up from nothing, look foolish!"

I started to sink in my seat. What on earth prompted this outburst? This is just one client, and a rather batty one at that. In my inexperience, I had assumed that Harry would take my side. Stupid me.

After letting him rant for a few minutes more, I finally found my voice, "Harry, why are you being this way? Look, I really need this job right now. Tell me how to fix things with Marcos."

"Well, you should have thought of that before you questioned him so harshly. I don't know if you can fix this. It might be too late. I could just kill you, Annie! I'm going to my room," he ground out. He threw a fifty on the table and got up. Before he left for his room at the inn, he added, "Stop by my room tomorrow morning before I leave. Be there at nine. Don't be late. I need to think more about this situation before we speak again." Harry's whole tone had shifted. He no longer sounded like a throwback to the '70s. No, now I thought he sounded more like a gangster from the '20s. I imagined him with his hair slicked back with spats on his feet. His words came rat-a-tat, as if he fired them from a machine-gun. A shiver went up my spine.

Turning around, he almost collided with the owner of the inn, Kitty Breckenridge. Lizzy had introduced Kitty and I earlier that afternoon, when I had wandered downstairs to take a brief break from this project. Standing almost as tall as me (which is not tall at all), Kitty had an elfin face with huge dark eyes. Her dark hair styled in a pixie haircut somehow matched her quick, bright movements. No fuss, no muss; Kitty seemed like a woman of action.

"Is everything okay, sir?" Kitty asked his retreating back. He never turned around. Either he didn't hear her, or he was that mad. Personally, I'd bet my money on the latter. She shifted her concern to me, "Are you okay, hon?"

I just stared at the table in disbelief. "Yeah, I think so," I said after a long pause. "You know, I don't think I'm the right girl for this project."

"What project?" Kitty asked, as she sat down with me. Discreetly, the waitress cleared away Harry's stuff, refilled my drink, and brought Kitty a new drink.

Grateful for a sympathetic ear, I unloaded the whole story on Kitty. Kitty listened attentively, asking questions occasionally. I wrapped it up by telling her that Lizzy and Janie knew most of the story, except for my last phone call with Marcos and, obviously, this dinner.

"What do you think I should do, Kitty? As a clearly successful businesswoman," I swept my hand over the bustling restaurant. "I really value your insight."

"You want my honest opinion?"

"Yeah."

"Run away from this project as fast as you can. Something seems off. I can't put my finger on it, but I don't like it. And, hey, if you need to do something different for a while, you can work here in the restaurant. Except for the week of Christmas, we are fairly busy with locals during the off-season. Plus I can include your room and board in your wages. But don't decide tonight. Sleep on it," Kitty said as she got up. She looked meaningfully at Harry's discarded fifty. She picked it up and handed it to me as she added, "Oh, and by the way, dinner's on me tonight." Winking, she left me to my thoughts.

Thanking her, I sighed and tried to figure out what to do. I decided I had no choice but to wait until my morning talk with Harry to make any decisions. The light of day might make everything clearer for me.

•••

I woke up determined to stick it out with the book. After all, I had signed a contract with Harry. Although I had no clue how to go about it, I needed to find peace with this project and make things right with Harry and Marcos. I certainly didn't understand this project, but I knew I could get through it. Somehow, I'd need to stick to really simple, boring questions and agree with whatever Marcos and Harry wanted for the book. Then, after the book was done, I'd either take the job with Kitty or... Hmm... I didn't have a Plan B. Well, I definitely did not want to ghostwrite another book. Ever. Again.

I made some coffee on the coffeemaker the inn supplied. Mmmm... nothing like the smell of Door County Cherry-flavored coffee. I had grown addicted to it during my short time up here. With the coffee safely brewing, I padded into the bathroom and got ready for the day. I put on a dressy white blouse, dark jeans, and black leather boots. There! I thought, dressy enough, but still casual. I threw on a bright scarf to top off the outfit. Now I was ready for the coffee.

In honor of my newfound resolve, I grabbed the marketing mug from the gift basket Harry had brought.

"Oof, wow, that's heavy," I muttered as I hefted up the ceramic mug. It felt like it weighed at least a couple of pounds. While preparing my coffee, I amused myself with the thought that the ceramic served as a great hiding place for a special microfiche. I imagined that any moment, spies would break through the door to commandeer the microfiche.

Shaking my head at my imagination, I told myself, "That's ridiculous! You've seen too many old movies. Besides, microfiche isn't that heavy."

Coffee gone, I glanced up at the clock. I squinted, hoping I read it wrong. Nope, it said 8:59. I had approximately one minute to hightail it to Harry's room. I wasn't really sure I remembered which room was his. It was either Room 3 or 5? Or maybe Room 6? I bit my bottom lip trying to recollect. Since I wanted grab more coffee and breakfast after our meeting, I grabbed my leather jacket, purse, and keys.

I dashed down the hall. I figured since I was in Room 4, I'd try 3 first since it was closest. I knocked lightly on the door. A giggling blonde in a white silk bathrobe opened the door. I could hear some male laughter in the background.

She greeted me, "Hi! Can we help you?"

"Come back to bed, honey!" I heard the guy say. He didn't sound like Harry, but I wasn't sure.

I didn't know where to look. Averting my gaze, I muttered, "Sorry to interrupt, but uh, is this Harry's room?"

Just then, the guy howled. The woman giggled again.

Noticing my increasing blush, she confided, "Don't mind him, we're on our honeymoon. I don't know anyone called Harry."

With that, she shut the door.

Sighing, I fanned my face in a sad attempt to cool down my red face. Fortunately, I got no response at Room 5, even after knocking really loudly. With my jaw set in determination, I made my way to what had to be Harry's room.

Previously, Lizzy had explained that Rooms 6 through 9 were on the third floor. I didn't see anyone on my way up the back stairs. The old inn had three floors total, four if you counted the basement. Because the inn had originally been designed as a gangsters' hideout, it had been expanded over the years, and the rooms were an eclectic hodge-podge of mazes. Some rooms were huge, with three rooms in a suite, whereas, other rooms were itty-bitty. When they bought the property, Kitty and Janie had decided to keep as many of the inn's original features as possible. As a result, many of the huge oak doors now guarded the inn's rooms like silent sentries. The upside was that the doors were huge and very thick; the downside was that they didn't seem to lock properly until you really pulled them shut (or forgot your keys).

At the top of the stairs, I checked the clock on my cell

phone. 9:03. I was late. Harry had distinctly said "don't be late." Racing down the hall, I frantically located his room. In my haste, I almost fell against the slightly ajar door. Stopping myself just in time, I knocked on the doorframe. "Harry?" I knocked a little louder. "Harry? Are you in there?" I asked, pushing the door open a little more. While I found it odd that the door was open, nothing with this project had been remotely predictable—why start now?

"Hello? Harry?" I called out tentatively, as I entered the room with my eyes closed. I had two motives: I didn't want to see him in his skivvies, and I really didn't want to startle him. Stepping inside Harry's room, I noticed how much it resembled an attic room and even had a gable window. With a window seat upholstered in striped shades of blue. Swallowing down my envy over the pretty room, my eyes swept the rest of the room. The southern-facing windows really brightened the room, bathing everything in warmth and sunshine (which did nothing to decrease my envy). Harry had lucked out view-wise, too. Since his room was on the third floor, he could see over the treetops to the shores of Lake Michigan, which was only a block from the inn. I noted Harry's watch on the nightstand, next to his reading glasses. He had his luggage arranged neatly in the corner and, presumably, today's outfit laid across an overstuffed chintz chair. Upon closer review, I espied the corner of an envelope sticking out of his suit jacket and wondered if that was my bonus check. Quickly, I strode across the room with the intention of…

"Miss! What are you doing?"

Of course—a maid would have to appear now. With a guilty start, I turned around to face one of Kitty's staff.

"I'm sorry, were you talking to me?"

"I don't see anyone else here, do I?"

I couldn't even fathom going through the whole story with her, so I made something up. I needed something to tell her, fast. Something that would justify being in Harry's room, without him.

"Oh, well, I'm just waiting for my lover, Harry." Lover? Oh my goodness, what had possessed me?

"Your lover?"

"Yes, yes, exactly. My lover. Harry and I became involved in a purely physical relationship the last time I went to Chicago, and he visited me this weekend." Pleased with myself, I smiled in smug satisfaction.

"Hmmm… then you'd better tell that blonde who visited his room last night that you are his lover," the maid shot back, putting an icky emphasis on "lover."

Reading her nametag, I cleared my throat nervously, "We have an open relationship. Anyway, what do you want, Millicent? Can I help you?"

Millicent eyed me suspiciously, "No, no. I was just getting a leg up on cleaning the rooms."

I felt a pang of guilt. Cleaning the whole inn, and without the benefit of an elevator, must be difficult. Millicent's untidy grey hair and imposing manner made her seem older than I thought, but the job would even be tough for a younger woman. Maybe that's why Millicent was so cranky. I vowed to cut her some slack.

I said, with a forced lightness, "Then you should probably get started. I'm sure Kitty's wondering where you are. I guess I'll go then, too. Harry must have gone to breakfast without me. That scamp!"

At the doorway, Millicent and I parted ways. Waiting until Millicent turned the corner, I scuttled back into the room and, again, tried to snag that envelope. However, something distracted me, and out of the corner of my eye, I saw a puddle of reddish-brown water on the bathroom floor. Reddish brown water? Determined to investigate, I walked across the room. With a sinking feeling, I called, "Harry? Hello? Are you in here?"

No answer. Tentatively, I entered the bathroom and saw the source of the puddle. Watery blood was running out of the bathtub and onto the floor, with Harry smack dab in the middle. My vision got very fuzzy and tunnel-like

as Harry's frozen face stared back at me.
I screamed.
Then, my world went black.

CHAPTER 8

WHEN I CAME TO, I SAW AT LEAST six faces hovering over me. Oh wait, the six faces became three. Three very concerned faces swam into focus. Kitty. Some cop. Oh, and a dreamy dark-haired fella. I smiled a little. At least I thought I did.

"Annie? Annie, what happened?"

"Are you okay?"

"Miss? Don't sit up too suddenly. You've had a shock."

Their voices were wrapped in gauze.

Suddenly, the memory of finding Harry's naked and very dead body came flooding back to me. I started screaming and tried to get up, only to be gently pushed back down by Donovan. Donovan? What was he doing in my bedroom?

And why was I swimming in my bedroom? I felt my wet sleeve. And realized my entire right side was wet. Ugh, gross.

"What happened?" I could hear Lizzy's voice as she approached the scene, as though it came from a tunnel.

"Hey Lizzy," I heard Kitty's distinctively smoky voice. "Don't worry, Annie's just in shock. We're not quite sure what happened, but we've called 911."

"911!" Lizzy sounded alarmed. "What on earth happened?"

"911! For me? I'm fine, though," I said, as I struggled to sit up. "Oof, that wasn't a good idea."

Blood rushed to my head and it throbbed.

"No, not for you. Well, partly for you, but mostly for the stiff in the tub." Kitty jerked her thumb towards Harry. Despite the situation, I almost laughed. Kitty had such an original way of sidestepping sentiment. Her practical outlook showed a woman who had a lot of life experience. Compared with my maudlin family, who tore out their hair about everything, I found it refreshing.

I saw Donovan gently steer some of the onlookers out of the bathroom and into the hallway, including the newlyweds. I heard snatches of their conversations.

"Did you see the naked man in the bathtub?"

"Did that girl who fainted know him?"

"Yes. I don't know."

"You know, she stopped by our room..." Straining to hear the rest over the drums beating in my head proved futile.

"Miss? Can you hear me?" the young police officer asked, worry creasing his brow. He looked very fair, with clear blue eyes. With his beefy build, I guessed he had probably been a linebacker on his high school football team.

I let out a huge sigh. "Yes, officer, I'm fine. A bit embarrassed and wet, but fine."

"Good. Good. I was just asking for your name, miss?"

"My name? Oh, right. I'm Annie Malone, er, Joanna Malone." I stuck out my hand for him to shake. Sheepishly, he shook my hand. I saw that his nametag said "Michaels."

"Gosh, I can see you're upset, Miss. But we do need you to give a statement."

"Yeah. Wait, what?" I put my head in my hands. When I looked up again, Officer Michaels was looking at me warily. He rubbed his left hand over the side of his face.

In the most melodramatic fashion I could, I held out my wrists with a bit of a flourish and said in dramatic, accented tones, "Very well, take me in."

"Seriously, Johnny. Why do you need to take Annie in? Can't you tell she's not the murdering type?" Kitty asked, quite reasonably in my somewhat biased opinion.

"Miss, put your wrists down. Everybody calm down! Annie is NOT, I repeat NOT, being arrested. And Kitty, with all due respect, I have orders to get a statement from the person who found the body. Annie, we do need you to come in and make a statement. Here's my card. We'll need to see you before the end of the day. Tomorrow at the latest."

"Oh." My voice sounded small as I realized the enormity of everything.

"Thank you for your cooperation, Kitty," said Officer Michaels as he left. "We'll be in touch. Sorry your regulars will have to miss your Packers' Sunday football party."

"Sure. Don't mention it," Kitty said as she waved to him. She didn't look that upset about closing down the bar and restaurant for a couple of days. Considering that she was typically open seven days a week, I figured she was glad for some time off, even if it was because of Harry's murder. Plus, she still had a few other paying guests in the inn.

A few minutes later, the paramedics finally came. They prepped the body for transport. One of the guys told Kitty I needed a mild sedative.

"I'm not sure. Let me see if I can find something downstairs. I'll be right back," and with that, Kitty left the room. Popping her head back in, she asked, "You mean some whiskey or something, right?"

The paramedic nodded.

Which left me alone with Harry, the paramedics, and my shock. My shock wasn't going anywhere anytime soon. I sank back to the floor and started to rock back and forth, hugging myself. In a pinched voice, I heard myself ask, "How come there isn't that much blood around?"

The paramedic explained that most of the blood went down the drain, which didn't help my shock at all.

When Donovan came back into the bathroom, he took one look at my pale face and dragged me downstairs. Well, based on how I felt, I can only assume that my face was pale. All I know is this, when he looked at me, he blanched a little himself.

"Where are we going?"

"The bar."

"The bar? It's only ten in the morning!"

"Pretend it's brunch and I'm making you a variation on a Bloody Mary, okay?" He added, "I think you need something a little stronger than soda. Do you think Kitty has any brandy at the bar?"

Still pulling me, we got to the empty bar. As a result, you could hear a pin drop.

Being away from Harry's lifeless body helped me a lot. I even cracked a little smile as we looked over Kitty's enormous liquor collection behind the bar, "I'm guessing she does. I think what she doesn't have would make a shorter list."

Donovan turned and smiled at me. "It seems your shock is fading. How's your head?"

"It's been better."

"Ah! Here it is!" Donovan grabbed a bottle and moved expertly behind the bar to pour me a snifter of brandy. He poured a pint of beer for himself.

"Do people know what happened?"

"Yeah, unfortunately."

I studied his face, noting that his nose was healing nicely. He only had a little butterfly bandage over its bridge. He had such a nice nose. So straight. Apparently, I was a nose person. Who knew? I giggled a little at my wandering thoughts. He looked at me quizzically, which made me snort a little. Charming. I figured I should probably apologize for my crazy behavior at Janie's shop. I opened my mouth to speak.

But he beat me to it. "I'm sorry about the other day."

"You? Why are you sorry? You were just being funny. I yelled at you. In. A. Store." I took a sip of brandy. Wow, that went down easy. The drink warmed me completely through (or it could have been how Donovan looked at me). I felt the color begin to return to my face.

"You were fine. You were just spooked, I get it. My sister would have done the same thing. Oh, and just to bring everything out in the open, you did $1600 in damage to my car the other day." He looked at me over his beer before he took a long drink.

For a second, I just stared at him, perplexed. I clenched my teeth and ground out, "Are you kidding me?"

I noticed the teasing twinkle in his eye the moment before he burst out laughing and said, "Oh my gosh, it is too easy with you! Nah, you did hardly any damage."

I started laughing too. Then I remembered Harry's corpse and stopped abruptly.

"What's wrong?" Donovan asked.

"I was just thinking about Harry and thought maybe I shouldn't be laughing. What with everything going on upstairs and all."

Donovan seemed to sober up a bit, too. "How well did you know him?"

"He was my editor."

"Oh, have you written a book?"

"A couple. I'm a ghostwriter for a vanity publishing house, so it isn't nearly as glamorous as it sounds. But this particular gig was really good." I frowned a little in thought.

"If it was so good, why are you making that face?"

"Well, my gut has been bugging me since I accepted this gig. And this mysterious death just makes me even more edgy."

"Aren't you kind of young to be writing books?"

"How old should I be?"

Donovan whispered, "I guess I'm asking if you can legally drink that brandy."

I whispered back, "Yeah, I get that a lot. No worries, I'm twenty-two. And as far as the writing goes, I write what they tell me to."

"Oh, by the way," Donovan made the hold on a second motion with his finger and walked over to his charcoal grey sports jacket. He pulled a white envelope out of the pocket and brought it to me. "I believe this is yours."

Donovan handed me an envelope that simply said, "Annie Malone, Bonus."

Opening the envelope, I exclaimed, "My five thousand dollars! Oh, thank you so much! Where did you get it?"

"Sure, no problem. I don't like to divulge my methods. Is that your normal pay?" He sounded impressed.

"Oh no. Between the higher-than-normal pay and now Harry's murder… I don't know what to make of this project. My guts are getting so tied up. This project just feels off." As I spoke, I noticed a sticky note on my check. Glancing at the note, it looked like an address. While Donovan took a sip, I slipped the note into my jacket pocket.

Still thinking about his Houdini tactics in getting my bonus, I figured he must have slipped into Harry's room while everyone was busy in the bathroom. I wondered if he had discovered anything else in Harry's room. Donovan seemed to have many layers to him. Interesting. Hey, how did my brandy fill up again?

"I see. May I ask what the book is about?"

"Sure." I gave Donovan the *Reader's Digest* version in between sips of brandy. At the mention of Marcos' name, I thought I saw a shadow flicker across his face. His eyebrow definitely twitched when I mentioned Tina Delvecchio. I made a mental note to ask him about that later. As I wrapped up the story, the paramedics came downstairs with the body.

"Interesting. So, had you ever met Harry before?"

Drinking the last of my brandy, I noticed my hands had stopped shaking. I looked at my face in the mirror behind the bar. My color had definitely returned.

"Annie, had you met Harry before this weekend?"

"What? Oh, I'm sorry. This brandy was the greatest idea! But to answer your question, no, I had not."

"I'm sorry that he was killed."

"Yeah, me too," I frowned as I said this. Was it my imagination (or the brandy) or was Donovan staring at me really intently? Why was he so interested in my relationship with Harry? Oh no, I hope Millicent didn't spread that stupid rumor about Harry being my lover! Stop it, Annie! You don't even know if Donovan thinks like that about you. Caught in my own thoughts, I put my brandy snifter down more forcefully than I intended. That seemed to clear my spiraling thoughts a little. With a flourish, I gestured towards the door.

"And now I should probably get going to the police."

"Do you know where it is? Ummm… why don't I give you a ride over there? You aren't really used to drinking much, are you?"

"I'm fine." Although as I said this, I stumbled a little, which didn't really make my case.

"You are that. But you are a little buzzed. In good conscience, I can't let you drive there. So, I'm ready whenever you are."

"Very well. We might as well go now. There's no time like the present. Drive on, Jeeves."

Before Donovan took me to the station, he said I had time to change. Leaving my purse and jacket with him, I ran up to my room and threw on dry, unstained jeans with my Packers long-sleeved t-shirt.

•••

Fortunately, it was a bit of a drive to the Door County police station in Michigan City. During the 25-minute drive, my buzz wore off completely, and Donovan turned on the Packers pregame show. I was relieved he did; I had always found sports commentaries oddly soothing, and I didn't feel like talking. I shut my eyes for most of the drive and just tried to relax, being lulled by the sports guys doing their thing.

As we approached Michigan City, I opened my eyes and started preparing myself mentally. Michigan City was the biggest city in the Door County peninsula. Actually, it was the only actual city on the peninsula. The other communities that dotted the peninsula were towns and villages. Michigan City had chain stores and fast food restaurants, a hospital, regular companies, and movie theaters—and provided many of the civic services offered to the rest of the peninsula. In my short time on the peninsula, I had learned it served as a kind of "guardian" to the northern section of the Door County peninsula.

We drove through downtown and reached the station. Donovan double-parked in front to let me out. Before I shut the door, I leaned into the car to thank Donovan for the ride and to find out where he wanted to pick me up when I finished. However, before I got a word out, he stopped me and said, "Hey Annie, I'm really sorry, I won't be able to give you a ride home."

"Oh, um, okay. I guess… well, um… are there cabs up here?"

"No need. Lizzy is going to bring you back. She's going to be here in about an hour to pick you up. I texted her while you were freshening up." He looked at my worried face and added, "And, hey, don't be nervous. I have a feeling everything is going to be just fine."

"Okay. Well, thanks for the ride here. I'll see ya around," I said before turning around and walking up the path.

Built in the late 1880s, the three-story square building

was red brick with white trim and white columns in front. Inside, the recently restored police station had marble floors and beautiful dark oak trim. I sniffed the air, and smelled lemon wood cleaner, disinfectant, and cigar smoke. Cigar smoke?

I told the receptionist who I was and why I was there. In a move right out of Psych Ops, I sat in the waiting room as the minutes ticked by on the clock above my head. After 30 minutes of waiting, someone entered the waiting area. Sure enough, it was Officer Michaels. He took me into a secure area behind a thick metal door. We entered the interrogation room.

"Okay, here's where I leave you. Just have a seat on the other side of the desk," said Michaels.

"By the mirror?" I asked nervously.

Michaels nodded. He told me a detective would be in shortly for my questioning. Enigmatically, he added, "I'm sorry," as he shut the door behind him.

"Sorry for wha—?" I began. I sighed and started gnawing on my lower lip. Michaels must not have heard me. I wondered what he could be sorry about. I knew I had plenty to be sorry about, especially after agreeing to take this book project.

CHAPTER 9

MY NERVES INCREASED AS I GOT closer to being questioned. Of course *I* knew I was innocent and they had said this was merely part of the procedure, but I had never been in this predicament before. I had purposely lived my life in such a way to NOT ever be questioned by the cops. I ran events through my head again. Ever since I had accepted this disastrous book contract, I had felt weird. I had felt like some unseen puppet master was controlling things from behind-the-scenes. Harry's murder did nothing to dispel that feeling. Humpf, I reasoned, the murder strengthened that feeling tenfold.

"Miss?" A gruff, baritone voice interrupted my thoughts. I looked up. And up. And up. A kind of giant with no neck stood before me. The harsh light gleamed off his Mr. Clean-like head. His beady eyes narrowed. "I'm Officer Chad Dupah and I'll be taking your statement regarding the death of Harry Scarpelli."

"Yes," I sighed. He had me state my name, birthdate, and temporary and permanent addresses. Then he began the interrogation.

"Okay, let's get started." He actually rubbed his hands

together.

I groaned in anticipation.

He scanned over the paperwork. "So, you killed a guy, huh?"

I lifted my chin a notch. "Pardon?"

"Oh, Little Miss-Innocent-As-Pie doesn't have an answer to that, does she?" He slammed his hands on the desk in front of me. His movement startled me, and I jumped a little. His upper lip sneered in amusement, "Where were you last night?"

Without even giving me a chance to answer, he goaded me, "Don't have an answer?"

"Of course, I have an answer. Number one, I didn't kill anyone. And number two, I went to dinner with my editor, Harry Scarpelli. At the Lighthouse Inn. Do I need to get a lawyer for this?"

"No need, no need. Just answer the questions and don't get lippy. Who saw you leave?"

"Who saw me leave? I'm staying there. Do you mean leave the dining room?"

"Don't answer my question with a question."

"Okay. Kitty saw me leave the dining room, and I went straight to my room."

"Well, I don't mean to nitpick, but who's to say you didn't sneak back up to Harry Scarpelli's room the minute Kitty's back was turned?" Chad threw up his hands in disgust. "I don't know what game you're playing, Joanna Malone. How do you know Marcos Landrostassis?"

At Marcos' name, I started. Why on earth would this detective bring up Marcos? "Marcos? How does he figure into this? Harry hired me, well Harry's publishing company hired me to write Marcos' book."

"You know him well? Are you, ah, 'working' with him?" Chad ran his finger along my cheek. Between him touching me and putting a weird emphasis on "working," I threw up a little in my mouth. My fingers itched to smack his big, giant chrome dome of a head. Someone knocked on the door. "Have you ever met Tina Delvecchio?" He stood up.

"Why did you kill Harry the Editor?" Chad yelled into my face. The knocking became more insistent. "I know you di—." The knocking grew very loud. "Oh, for goodness sake. Hold on just a sec, Little-Miss-Perfect."

I rolled my eyes when he turned to answer the door.

"Whaddya want anyway?" Chad rudely asked as he threw open the door.

A uniformed officer entered the room and urgently whispered something in Chad's ear. I longed to know what he said, especially because of what followed.

Chad looked extremely agitated. The officer stayed in the room, clearly waiting for Chad to do something.

Chad paced the room a few times, then turned around and faced me, "You can go. But don't leave town anytime soon!"

"What?"

"Apparently, you have some powerful friends. Get out of here."

I didn't hesitate. I grabbed my jacket and purse and didn't look back until my feet hit pavement. I took in several gulps of crisp fall air. What the heck was all that about anyway? Is that how routine questioning was conducted? Wasn't that supposed to just be routine questioning? And who was my powerful "friend"? I didn't know very many people up here. All these questions and more ran through my head.

"Don't leave town." The detective's words echoed through my head. Why couldn't I leave town? From the mystery novels that I've read, the plucky heroine (who I guess would be me?) is only told to not leave town when she is a suspect! A suspect? Me? Moi? As far as I could see, my only crime was asking Marcos the question, "Why?"

In a daze, I left the cop shop and walked straight out into traffic. I only came to when I heard Lizzy honking repeatedly at me.

"Hey!" Lizzy hung out her car window and yelled, "Annie! Over here!"

"What?" I turned and started walking towards her. A Jeep Wrangler almost clipped my hand as I turned. "Gosh, what the what?!" Babying my injured hand, I made my way to Lizzy's Honda CR-V.

"What'd they say? Who questioned you?"

"They told me I couldn't leave town!"

"Really?" Lizzy scrunched up her nose. "That's crazy! Anyone would take one look at you and know you couldn't kill anybody!"

"I know, right?! I don't know what to do."

"Well... hop in. We'll figure it out."

"Where are we going anyway? I'm not sure I can sit alone in my room right now."

"Then you, my dear new friend, are in luck." Lizzy expertly pulled back into traffic, "I hope you don't mind, I took the liberty of getting us invited to Janie's for the game, appetizers, and adult beverages. Kitty is coming up too. Since the Lighthouse Inn has to be closed, she figured we should at least enjoy our time off. And she figured you needed a break."

Glumly, I nodded.

Lizzy looked over at me and smiled a little bit, "Hey, I know things look grim, but you have the truth on your side. Too bad you didn't have that hot Donovan guy as an alibi!"

Despite myself, I cracked a smile. One of the best ways to recognize a friend for life is someone who can make you smile even when the chips are down.

"He is crazy-hot, isn't he?" I whispered. Since I looked more like the sidekick than the heroine, guys tended to overlook me. I couldn't tell whether Donovan thought of me as a potential friend, or more than that. I also couldn't tell if I hoped he thought of me as more than that. I did know that he messed up my frequency when he was nearby, and made my knees knock. I shook my head to clear out any cobwebs.

"Do you need to let off some steam tonight?"

"More than you know. I feel like I've been through the wringer! Some Chad-jerk guy questioned me. Do you know him?"

"Bald?"

"Check."

"Bad attitude?"

"Check."

"Sneer?"

"Check."

"You might say I know him. You might say I used to date him."

"You dated that Neanderthal? Why?"

"Youth and stupidity. Believe me, I learned my lesson quickly." Lizzy shook her head in amazement, "Wow— you got stuck with Chadwick interviewing you? You're lucky you got out of there in one piece. Either he's slipping or he has a soft spot for you!"

"That's a soft spot? Ai yi yi, coulda fooled me! I'd hate to see him with someone he didn't like!"

Lizzy threw back her head and laughed, "Yeah, that's a long list. We'll fill you in on his story at Janie's. It's a good one!"

I started to lighten up a little as we drove up the highway to Janie's townhouse in Turtle Bay. The crisp fall air, and listening to the start of the Packers game, did wonders for my mood. Plus, since Lizzy drove, I got to really enjoy the gorgeous fall colors. On the way down to the police station, I had been too nervous to enjoy the drive. I should still be nervous, right? I had a sneaking suspicion that my nerves were more affected by Donovan than I'd care to admit.

•••

"So, is it true you actually found the body, Annie?" Janie asked during a break in the game. I nodded and held up my finger as I finished eating a chicken wing. "Mmmmm, these are great! What's your recipe?"

Janie delicately lifted an eyebrow. "Is that your way of letting me know you don't want to talk about...," her voice dropped to a whisper, "you know?"

Kitty and Lizzy stared at me, waiting for my answer. I had a feeling that my new friendships hung a little in the balance based on my answer. They needed me to trust them. And we hadn't talked about the elephant in the room yet. When Lizzy and I first got there, the Packers game was in full swing so I got a bit of a reprieve (yes, in Wisconsin, even women pay close attention to football games). Plus, Janie and Kitty had put out quite a party buffet, so we were busy eating and drinking. I suspected that Kitty had brought a lot of the food they had prepared for the Lighthouse Inn's now-defunct game party. Regardless of where the food came from, their kindness and friendship touched me very deeply. What happened next might have been the drinks or the emotional upheaval in my life, but it bonded the four of us.

I looked up to find Janie giving me an odd, searching look, her dark brown eyes bearing down deep into my eyes. To be honest, it freaked me out a little bit. Although Janie and Kitty didn't look at all like sisters, I found that they both seemed to have the ability to see into a person's soul. Right now, I felt like Janie saw things that no one else could have seen. I found it disconcerting, yet oddly soothing. However, it also brought everything I had felt in the last week very close to the surface.

To my horror, I burst into tears. Sobs wracked my body, as I tried to talk, "I'm sorry... this is-is-is-isn't l-l-l-like m-me." I felt the wind shift in the room as my new friends gathered around me.

I heard a chorus of "there, there" and "it's okay."

With gratitude, I accepted a tissue and glass of wine

that Janie offered me. In one gulp, I downed the wine.

"Hmmm... you must have needed that," Lizzy said as she deftly took my empty glass. "Do you feel a little better?"

I nodded. "Yeah, I've just been through a lot in the last week or so." I blew my nose loudly. "Thanks, guys."

"Well, you did find a dead body today," Kitty wryly observed as she nibbled on a chip loaded with spinach artichoke dip. "Have another glass, sweetie." She filled up my glass again.

"That isn't even the half of it," cried Lizzy. "Our poor Annie got interviewed by none other than Chadwick!"

"Oh no! Not Chad!"

"Tsk! Tsk! That's too bad!"

While Kitty and Janie exclaimed over my bad luck at finding Harry, then being interviewed by Chad, Lizzy brought me another plate of wings and chips with dip. I thanked her as I accepted the plate.

"And you guys know I didn't kill Harry, right?"

A chorus of "Of courses" echoed.

However, I didn't miss the look that Janie and Kitty shared with each other. I resolved to not let it bother me at this point. They didn't know me well—it was only natural that they were wary.

Besides, I was starting to formulate an idea of my own. Since Lizzy and I had become such unusually fast friends, I planned to talk to her the next day about us trying to find Harry's killer. In the meantime, the four of us enjoyed a resounding Packers win, then another bottle of wine. With the additional wine, some of the courage I had recently lacked came rushing back.

"So what can you guys tell me about this Chad Dupah? His questioning technique really lacked subtlety."

Lizzy nodded. "Even though I wasn't in school with them at the same time, I remember hearing how Chad and his buddies were terrors in high school. Of course, I had the misfortune of dating him until Janie and Kitty helped me out of that jam. Janie, you were Chad's year, weren't you?"

Janie's eyes lit up as she warmed to her topic. "Chad has always been a huge weasel. I'm really not surprised his questioning methods lacked subtlety. That man doesn't have a subtle bone in his body."

"Janie, tell Annie what happened to Chad the summer of your senior year." added Kitty.

"What happened? I'm really curious. He came across as such a jerk today."

"Let me see if I remember it in the correct sequence," Janie said, tapping her chin. She took a big swig of wine. "Okay, if I recall correctly, a bunch of us kids were at the beach, you know, just hanging out and having fun. We stayed at the beach into the night. Anyway, at about midnight a bunch of kids decided to go skinny-dipping (not me, I might add, wink wink), but at the last minute they changed their mind because the cops were rumored to be on their way. But Chad was the only one they forgot to tell. He had gotten in the water before anyone else, and must have been swimming underwater when people started to leave. Anyway, in the rush to leave, someone accidentally grabbed his clothes, so he was left without any… ahem… covering, as it were."

"Did the cops take him in?"

Janie shook her head. "Well, that's just it. The cops never came. And since his car keys were in his pants pocket, he was stuck walking home."

"In the buff?" I exclaimed.

Janie nodded. "Yep. But that isn't the worst. It's how he retaliated that made the situation so awful."

"He wasn't cool about it?"

"Did the man you met strike you as someone who would be cool and let it go?"

"No, not really. What did he do?" I leaned forward in the chair.

"He threw rotten eggs on the cars of the kids who had

abandoned him.'"

"You're kidding!"

"Nope, I would not kid about that. And you know what dried egg does to paint, right?"

Wide-eyed, I nodded. "So he has a bit of a vengeful streak? I mean it isn't like they did it on purpose."

"And he has to have the last word."

"Great combination," Lizzy wryly observed. "Yep, he's the whole package all right."

Janie gave Lizzy a funny look and burst into gales of laughter. After a few seconds, we were all struck by Lizzy's wording and all four of us were in tears from laughing so much.

Gasping for air, Kitty said between laughs, "That's what she said," which just got us going even more. Between the visual of Chad bopping down the darkened country roads in his birthday suit and Kitty's comment, it took us quite a while to stop laughing.

Once we had settled down, Lizzy and I offered to help clean up the party before leaving.

"Nonsense," said Janie. "Kitty will stay and help. Both of you go and get a good night's sleep."

Lizzy and I hugged them good-bye at the door and headed out to Lizzy's truck. Dusk approached as we drove down the highway, back to the Lighthouse Inn. I loved the feeling of dusk—the sense of snugness and comfort.

Just before she dropped me off, Lizzy turned to me and asked, "So, are you sure you'll be okay by yourself?"

"Oh sure, I'll be fine. The party helped," I said, getting out of the car. "Thanks again!"

I hesitated and motioned for Lizzy to wait and roll down the window. "Also, I made a decision. Would you mind meeting me for lunch tomorrow?"

"Sure, sounds mysterious." Lizzy smiled and waved as she drove away.

CHAPTER 10

PATIENCE WAS NEVER MY STRONGEST characteristic. I preferred to act first and ask questions later, but now I didn't know what to do. I did know that my name needed clearing. Unemployed. Possibly suspected of murder. Almost-but-not-quite-broke. I knew two things: 1. I needed to clear my name of suspicion. 2. I needed to know the status of this book—immediately. I mean, I had a nice little bonus to live on for a bit, while I tried to figure out what to do. I needed to find out whether this book was still going forward.

For the umpteenth time that evening, I tried to call Marcos to find out what was happening with the book since Harry's murder. And for the umpteenth time, the phone rang and rang. I expected voicemail to kick in or something, but it didn't. That struck me as very peculiar. I held out hope for about ten rings, then gave up. At this point, I didn't even know if Marcos knew that Harry was dead.

As I hung up the phone, I went over my dinner with Harry yet again. He had been a grade-A jerk, but I realized he must have been worried about something. Maybe he was anxious that he had been followed? He had always been pretty nice on the phone. I had a hard time reconciling his behavior to me in person. I decided to write down the timeline of events and do some investigating on my own. Could it have been a random theft and killing? I wondered that, but hit a wall upon the remembering that nothing seemed to have been taken (except, of course, the bonus check that had my name on it, which Donovan had grabbed for me). The whole project had seemed fishy from the beginning. I mentally kicked myself for ignoring my gut. It seemed like every time I ignored my instincts, I didn't just get blindsided, I got hit by a Mack truck.

It hadn't even helped when I had called Grandpa and Aunt Helen to fill them in on events. I really didn't want them to find out via the news, which might make it down to Milwaukee since it entailed murder. Although I should have realized it ahead of time, my call only increased their worry for me. It didn't help that I was still a little fuzzy-headed from the wine at Janie's impromptu party.

"So, what are you going to do job-wise?" my Grandpa had asked. I imagined him sitting with his buddy, Joe McNulty, at the kitchen table with a steaming mug of coffee and an overflowing plate of Aunt Helen's delicious cookies.

I shrugged, which he couldn't see over the phone. Then, taking a sip of my diet soda, I tried to alleviate his concern (with a bravado I did not feel), "I still might have the book to do. Otherwise, I dunno." I tried to avoid telling them that I'm under suspicion for murder. Since I was innocent until proven guilty, it seemed like borrowing trouble to mention that.

"Yeah, well, you need to find out what's going on, I think," Grandpa agreed. "Do they have any idea who did it?"

I could hear Aunt Helen in the background. "What happened, Frank? Is Annie okay?"

"Hold on a sec, Anna Banana," Grandpa said, then

covered the phone. I could hear muffled sounds as he tried to explain, in just a few seconds, about me finding Harry.

Aunt Helen's shout of "Annie found a body!" came through loud and clear. So did the thud when she fainted. I guess it runs in the family.

Not shocking, the next sound I heard was Grandpa's brief "Good-bye" as he got off the phone to tend to Aunt Helen. Whew! Now, I only had to hope that I could clear my name before talking to him again.

That duty done, I grabbed my timeline, stuffed it in my jeans' pocket, and left for the restaurant down the road. I wasn't really hungry, but I needed to be around people. My knees quaked from nerves at the thought of this crazy situation I had fallen into, but I was hopeful that my name would be cleared.

So, I threw on my leather jacket and grabbed my purse, and hoped for the best as I left my room. I had seen a funky little Mexican cantina-style restaurant down the street from the Lighthouse. I figured I'd hunker down at the bar there and maybe have a margarita. Or two. Or three. Well, probably, not three... I didn't have much tolerance for alcohol. In all honestly, even two seemed a little high for me.

•••

Apparently, the Packers win hadn't been enough to kick this story to the curb on the Sunday night news. I got to the cantina just as they aired the press conference on Harry's murder. I guess (thankfully), not many people get killed in Door County, so it was major news.

Unfortunately, they did show a picture of me as a possible suspect. I cringed. Where did they get that picture? I looked like a homeless person. I really needed to rethink my wardrobe choices. Oh, and I needed to jumpstart my efforts to find Harry's killer (probably the bigger priority, right?).

One of the bar patrons happened to turn around and see me right after the report. He piped up, "Hey! You're the girl from the news report!"

Then I heard a chorus of:

"You didn't do it, did you?"

"What did he do to you to make you so mad?"

"Should we call the cops?"

I looked around the room in horror. I really hadn't expected this kind of reaction. Being a peaceable kind of person, I typically didn't behave badly and, as you know, I don't like being the center of attention. Plus, killing someone didn't even register remotely on my radar. So, I was in very unpleasant territory and had no idea what to do.

"C'mon, guys! I don't even own a gun!" I tried to shout over the din.

A woman sporting a mullet shouted out, "So, was it a crime of passion?" I turned bright red. Mullet-head looked at the guy who started it all, "Wilbur, just look at how red she is!"

"Irene! How could you think that! Just look at her! She can't be older than 15!" said the apparent ring-leader, Wilbur.

Suddenly, I heard Millicent join the cacophony, "Actually, she told me that they were lovers." Kitty's maid would have to pipe up with that false tidbit.

Inwardly I groaned. I tell one little white lie to get me out of an awkward situation and it comes back to slap me. Typical.

I wasn't sure if I should stay and defend myself or flee with my tail between my legs. It wasn't like I had been arrested or read my Miranda rights, but I probably shouldn't talk about this in public. Who knew who could be listening? I decided to split the difference and sat down to order a drink. I figured if I didn't give in to their questions, they'd let up eventually.

An older couple in their seventies sat next to me at the

bar. The man had white hair with a bit of a stooped back, and I was struck by the mischievous glint in his eyes. The lady smiled at me and reached over him to pat my hand.

"There, there, dear," the lady said sympathetically. "It sounds like you've been through quite a bit today."

I smiled back at her. "Oh, I'll be okay. I just feel bad for Harry. Not a good way to die." The bartender came by, and I gave my order of a double strawberry margarita. Before I got served, he had to verify my age on my driver's license. No worries there, since I had been drinking legally for over a year. I noticed that the other patrons had started to ignore me already.

"I'm Edgar and this is my wife, Marian," said the old man. We shook hands and I formally told them my name.

"Well, you seem to have the right attitude," said Edgar. "Don't let this crowd upset you. They're half in the bag anyway."

"Oh yes, most of the older people in Brook Harbor come here every night."

"So, it's kind of like that show, *Cheers*?" My margarita appeared in front of me and I settled the bill right away.

"You could say that," said Marian.

At that moment, all eyes turned to the entrance and, as if on cue, everyone yelled out "Doc!" Yep, completely like *Cheers*, and apparently Doc was their "Norm." I watched as this older gentleman with a full head of curly white hair and wire glasses raced to take his spot at the bar. The bartender immediately brought him a glass of something clear and a twist of lemon. Wait? Was the glass engraved with "Doc"? Wow—now that was a bar regular!

"What does Doc drink anyway?" I asked, trying to take my mind off my troubles.

"Double gin," said Edgar.

"Oh, yes, he has it every night. At least a couple of them. His insides must be a tinderbox. As for myself, I stick with good old-fashioned martinis." With that, Marian gave a demure hiccup.

"So, did you do it, anyway?" asked Edgar.

Marian gave Edgar a light slap on his wrist, then hiccupped again. "You can't ask that, honey. Besides, does our new little friend, Annie, look like she could murder anyone? She looks like she's not even out of high school." Fortunately, the margarita was having its effect and I didn't mind Edgar's question too much.

"Well, I don't know. No, I don't really think so," said Edgar sheepishly. "He might have pulled some funny business on Annie. I think if she did do it, it would be some kind of self-defense thing. You don't really know what any person might do to defend themselves."

Marian let out a huge sigh. "Okay, let's change the subject. Say, Annie, how long will you be up in Door County?"

"I'm not sure yet. But I really love it up here."

"What did you come up here for?"

I explained my ghostwriting project and how Harry figured into it. I noticed they both looked startled when I mentioned Marcos Landrostassis by name.

Not wanting to pounce on them, I casually asked them if they knew Marcos.

"Well, um, no, not really," started Edgar.

"That is to say, we don't really know him but we know of him," said Marian. "And, let me tell you, I never would have thought—"

At that moment, a karaoke contest started on stage and someone came by and dragged Marian to the stage mid-sentence.

Edgar good-naturedly laughed, "Sorry about that, Annie. They go way back, and Harriet loves to make Marian sing 'Working 9 to 5' with her during the karaoke contests.

"Huh, well, I guess every Lucy needs her Ethel," I observed, smiling back. Edgar slapped his knee and let out a howl in reply. I didn't think it was that funny, but I'd take it.

Marian and Harriet were the first duo up, and truth be told, they weren't too bad. Best of all, they looked like they were having fun. Edgar clearly enjoyed watching his wife rock out to Dolly Parton's hit.

Before I left, I finished my drink and made an Irish exit.

CHAPTER 11

"ANNIE, PLEASE DON'T THINK I'M crazy. But I have an idea..." Lizzy exclaimed as she burst into my room at eight the following morning. She dropped her handbag on the chair and plopped down on the couch. "I know we were supposed to meet for lunch, but I couldn't wait to run my idea by you, especially since it concerns you."

I looked at her with alarm. Who could blame me? She hadn't knocked and I had just showered and only wore my fuzzy yellow bathrobe and bunny slippers (so sue me... I loved my bunny slippers). I gaped at her through the wet hair hanging in my eyes.

"Do I need to be alert for this?" I asked, warily. I may have grunted a little, too.

"Oh, do you need caffeine to get started in the morning? Let's run across to the Chocolate Cow and get you some caffeine. I'll fill you in then." Lizzy shooed me back into the bathroom, saying, "Hurry up, then we can go. I'll wait for you out here. Do you have anything I can read?"

Briefly I popped my head out of the bathroom and nodded towards the nightstand. Lizzy followed my gesture and pounced on the newest Gretchen Archer book. One of the things we had bonded so quickly over was our mutual adoration of Ms. Archer, and mystery novels.

By the time she completed the first chapter, I reappeared with my hair done (er, kind of—does a messy ponytail count?), eyes lined, and clothes donned. We headed across the street to the Chocolate Cow and the best coffee on the Door Peninsula. The coffee-slash-fudge shop sat on the edge of the Harbor View Park, which lived up to its name. Even in cold mid-October, the harbor gave a great view of the bay and near-empty harbor.

As we stood in line at the Chocolate Cow, I asked Lizzy, "So, what's your idea? What did you want to dis-?" I stopped as Lizzy made the universal "STOP NOW!" sign of pretending to slash her throat. She mouthed "not here" to me. Then, I think she mouthed "wait till the moose slides," but that didn't make any sense. I figured I'd ask her again, outside.

Once we ordered our coffees, we trooped back out into the cold. Wishing I had brought my gloves, I held on to my hot coffee cup for warmth. I could see my breath. It was only mid-October and already morning temps were below freezing.

"So, what's this about 'wait till the moose slides'?" I asked, scrunching up my nose in confusion.

"Why would we wait till the moose slides? I don't even think we have moose up here."

"That's what I want to know."

"Why?"

"Why did you say that?"

"When did I say that?"

I could see we were getting nowhere with this circular conversation. I stopped walking. "When we were in the coffee shop, you mouthed 'wait till the moo-'..."

Lizzy's laughter interrupted me, then she said, "Oh, I'm sorry. I mouthed, 'wait till we're outside.'"

Once she calmed down after sending me into giggles

along with her, Lizzy explained, "I think we should find Harry's killer ourselves!"

I turned to her in surprise. "I was thinking the exact same thing! And I was worried you'd think I was crazy!" The caffeine had started to kick in, and Lizzy's announcement made me feel better than I had in days (well, not counting my meetings with Donovan, although those didn't make me feel good as much as they made me feel alive). "But I was afraid to ask, I didn't want to impose. I mean, you, Kitty, Janie, and Don-..." I felt a blush creep up my cheeks.

Lizzy pounced on my comment, "And Donovan?" At my wordless nod, she smiled. "Yeah, the way he looks at you. Wow!"

I was so tongue-tied, I couldn't even speak for several minutes.

Finally, I said, "Do you know how we go about this?"

"About what? Oh, the investigation? Sure, how hard can it be, right? We just tail a couple people, ask some nosy questions, and show up that dope Chadwick. Easy-peasy!" Lizzy made a "Voila!" gesture with her hands, forgetting she was holding a cup of coffee. The coffee cup and its contents went sailing through the air.

We both turned around and watched in horror as it landed with a splat on a nearby jogger. The woman, who had been gaining on us from behind, was dripping in coffee and whipping cream. Oh, and she gave us a big scowl. Fortunately, the coffee she wore had cooled off enough to not scald her, and Lizzy had drunk about half of it. But spilled coffee is spilled coffee, and the cold air didn't help matters.

Lizzy gasped and raced up to the irate runner. "Oh my! I'm so so sorry!" Towering over the petite jogger at her full five feet ten inches, Lizzy nearly knocked her over in her rush to help. The jogger stayed silent and continued to scowl.

Looking up momentarily after pulling some tissues

from her pocket, Lizzy realized that the jogger was Cindy Devlin. Cindy was a waitress and the newest member of Kitty's staff. Kitty had hired her in August when one of the servers quit, partly as a favor to Millicent the Unpleasant, Cindy's aunt. Because of Cindy's connection to Millicent, Kitty hadn't let her go at the end of the tourist season.

"Hey, Cindy, I didn't recognize you with that black hat pulled over your hair! I'm so sorry! Annie, do you have any napkins? Sometimes I gesture wildly when I talk. I guess I forgot I was holding a cup of coffee. Oh wow! Let me get your jacket washed. Can I do that for you?" Apparently, where I blushed when embarrassed, Lizzy chattered relentlessly.

I put my hand on Lizzy's arm to get her attention, and hand her the napkins I had fished out of my pocket.

Cindy's scowl lessened. A little bit. Through clenched teeth, she said, "It's okay. I'm fine." Lizzy kept trying to wipe the coffee off her. "Stop. It. Is. Fine," she ground out. Finally, when Lizzy tried to wipe her knit cap, Cindy lost it. "Leave me ALONE! I said I'm FINE. JUST. STOP. IT!"

I whispered to Lizzy, "Isn't there a restaurant up the road? Let's get the heck outta here! Plus, I'm starving!"

Unable to speak, Lizzy just nodded as I dragged her away. She looked like a bobble-head doll as we hightailed it to the Rise n' Shine Restaurant. Once we got seated, we just stared at each other and started laughing.

"What was that?" asked Lizzy, wiping tears from her eyes. "I feel bad about spilling the coffee. But it hardly justified THAT reaction!"

"I know! She totally freaked out! What's up with her hat anyway?" I said as we opened our menus. "Ooo… look at this menu. Everything looks amazing."

When the server came, we ordered more coffee. I ordered the Swiss cheese and spinach omelet. Lizzy opted to drown her coffee-spilling sorrows with their cherry-stuffed French toast.

I reopened the investigation discussion, "So, did you mean it? Do you really want to investigate Harry's murder with me?" The server brought our coffees.

Lizzy prepared her coffee and passed me the fake sugar and cream for mine. "Yes, and I think we need to start right away. Today even. I'm still off since Kitty can't open."

"She still can't? That's a shame. Have they given her any idea of when?"

"Probably tomorrow. At least I hope tomorrow. I need to make some money. I have got to get out of my sister's place soon. Before I kill her. Which brings me to the matter at hand. Let's talk murder!" With that, Lizzy pulled a notebook out of her inside jacket pocket. "Let's start at the beginning."

As if the restaurant had coordinated it with us, the server brought our food at that moment. We waited until she left, then Lizzy said, "Proceed."

"Okay, it all started about a week ago when…" and I told her the entire story. I talked between bites and she wrote between bites. An hour and three full cups of coffee later, we were through. Then I told her about my outing at the Mexican restaurant, including how quickly people went after me. We gathered the check and our jackets and made our way to the cash register.

"So, do you think this Tina Delvecchio is important?" Lizzy asked.

"I'm not sure, but that Chad detective-guy did ask me about her." Suddenly, I remembered something else and pulled Lizzy into a corner. My eyes grew wide and I grabbed Lizzy's arm, "You know what else? Donovan flinched a little when I mentioned Tina Delvecchio!"

"Ssh, try to keep your voice lower. People talk in these small towns," Lizzy hissed, "as you well know."

"Oops, sorry." I hung my head. I had gotten a swift course in Small Town Gossip 101 only the day before.

Lizzy waved her hand. "No worries. But why would Donovan flinch when you mentioned her?"

I shrugged. I didn't understand men and when I was as attracted to one as I was to Donovan, my wiring got screwed up. Therefore, I had no idea why he flinched, per se, but I do know it made me feel uncomfortable and slightly suspicious of him. Oh, who was I kidding? At this point, I was becoming suspicious of everyone. Well, almost everyone.

As if reading my thoughts, Lizzy said, "Doesn't this whole thing make you wary of people? I mean, how much do we really know about each other? I grew up here and I'm starting to really look at people differently."

Solemnly, I nodded in agreement. "Do you think Jim Donaldson is important?"

"Maybe." She shrugged. "I mean, he was Marcos' lawyer, right? Maybe you should call him, but I'd wait."

We paid our bill and left the restaurant. On our way back to the Lighthouse Inn, I had a brainwave.

"I think I know where we can start!" I said. "I can't believe I didn't think of it earlier!"

"What? What's your plan?"

I leapt in front of Lizzy and grabbed her arm, startling her. "We have an address!"

"How?" She kicked a little pile of fallen leaves on the sidewalk.

Without revealing how I got it, I told Lizzy that the address was on a sticky note inside the envelope with my last check from Harry. Since the project was probably over, I figured my bonus check was actually my last check. And since it was a pretty good amount, I figured I could coast for a bit while we searched for Harry's killer.

Pulling it out of my coin purse, I showed Lizzy the address. "It must be Marcos' address. I hadn't been given his address and I really wanted to talk to him. Harry's murder was as good a reason as any to find Marcos. This might be a good place to start our investigation," I said as I handed the note to her.

She handed it back to me with a weird look on her face. "I do not recognize this address at all."

"Hmmmm. I think Harry had said that Marcos lived near a winery. Do you know where that is?"

"Have you noticed how many wineries are up here? Oh well, we'll find it, somehow."

Parting ways at the Lighthouse Inn, we agreed that I would pick her up at her sister's house. Since her sister lived north of Brook Harbor, it made more sense for me to get her on the way to Marcos' address. Well, I wasn't certain it was Marcos' place, but who else's could it be, right?

CHAPTER 12

THREE HOURS LATER, WE WERE on our way to start the investigation.

Per the directions I had Googled, I turned onto a side street about a mile inland from Turtle Bay. Fortunately, Lizzy had recognized the winery right away, so we knew we were on the right track. As the road narrowed, the houses got bigger. By the time we reached the mystery house, the road had become a lane and the homes looked like mini-castles. Most of the houses had about two acres. The address we sought boasted a beautiful Tudor mini-mansion with no grass, indicating in-process landscaping. They had better get cracking, because the first snow usually fell in early-November in Northern Wisconsin.

"Do you think this is the place?" Lizzy whispered, clearly awestruck.

I could only nod. This place had to have 10 bedrooms. At the very least. A thousand questions swirled in my head. The main ones were: Why was this address in Harry's things? Who owned this house? Why were they landscaping in October? And, last but not least, if this was Marcos' house, how did he pay for it? Oh, wait, I thought of another one: Whose Cadillac Escalade sat in the horseshoe driveway? Not content to sit and wait for these answers to come to us, Lizzy and I went to the front door and rang the bell. No answer.

"Maybe it's broken. Wait, did you see that, Annie?"

"See what? Maybe we should knock." I lifted my hand accordingly.

"That!" Lizzy yelled. I looked up just in time to see an upstairs curtain flutter.

"Oh good, that just means someone is home. I'm sure they'll be down any minute to let us in," I said. My voice rose nervously with each syllable.

The golden-orange canopy of leaves, while beautiful, gave an eeriness to the whole situation. While there weren't a lot of homes on this lane, they seemed oddly quiet. I felt a shiver go down my back.

"Do you feel creeped out?" Lizzy squeaked.

"Look, we have a job to do," I boldly stated. Er, it would have sounded bold if my voice hadn't gone up an octave by the end of that statement. My knocking knees also betrayed me. I banged on the door more loudly.

"Hello?" I yelled at the door. "Hello-o-o!"

"I'm just gonna go around back and see if there's another door," Lizzy said, pointing her thumb over her shoulder. I nodded, intent on the task I had set myself.

A few minutes later, I had nothing to show for my efforts but sore knuckles. Suddenly, I heard a loud crash and a muffled, "Help! Annie! Come quick!"

I ran around the house but didn't see Lizzy anywhere. Turning around in circles, I called out, "Lizzy, where are you?"

"Down here," came her still-muffled reply. I saw her hand pop up out of the ground. She waved.

I walked to where I saw her hand and found her in a hole dug into the ground. "Wow, good thing you're tall. I don't think my hand would have reached."

She replied, somewhat impatiently, "Can you help me

up, please?" She made a spitting sound. A wad of dirt came flying out of her mouth.

As I was about to bend down and offer her my hand, we heard a truck start. Together we cried, "The Escalade!"

Our eyes locked and she shooed me away, "Go, go, see who that is! I'll be fine."

Lizzy had barely gotten the words out before I unceremoniously released my hand. I heard her tumble back down, but knew I had to hurry. Besides, she was tall; if she could just get a foothold, she'd be out of the pit in no time.

Racing back around the house, I got there just in time to see the Escalade peel out (as much as an Escalade can). Leaves and dirt flew everywhere. However, before my vision was obscured by flying debris, I saw a blonde head over the driver's seat. Seconds later, Lizzy came running up, covered head to toe in dirt, twigs, and leaves. We must have made quite a sight!

"Did you see who that was?" she asked, still panting from her efforts.

"All I could see was a blonde." Cough. Hack… "head." I coughed so hard, I thought my lungs would pop out. "I think I swallowed some dirt."

"Swallowed some dirt? I'm a walking mud pie!" Lizzy's voice steadily grew to a shriek as she spoke. She began to gesture rather wildly, whipping dirt over everything, including me.

"I don't even know what happened! I was walking along, looking for any signs of life, and BAM, I fell into that pit! I had thought it was a pile of leaves. But noooooo! It couldn't be a pile of leaves. It had to be a booby trap! Who booby traps their backyard for goodness' sake?"

"Hmmm… I wonder why they built a pit in their backyard?"

"I can certainly tell you why. I think they're up to no good here." Lizzy and I started at the unexpected voice behind us. We turned around and saw an old woman, who

I presumed was a neighbor.

"Who lives here?" I pointed towards the house.

"Don't know. But they have strange comings and goings all day and night," she said in a scratchy voice. Reaching just over five feet, I rarely felt tall next to people. Next to this lady, I felt positively gigantic. Lizzy easily stood a full foot taller than her. Wearing a pink cardigan, blue polyester pants, and tan orthopedic shoes, all she lacked was a Bingo card in her hand.

"What do you want with them anyway?" She squinted at us suspiciously through her Coke bottle glasses. "You up to no good, too?"

"No, no, not at all," Lizzy exclaimed. She held up her hands and made a placating motion.

"We are up to good, actually," I said. "We were wondering if we could ask you some questions about this house? Do you have a few minutes? I'm Annie Malone and this is my friend, Lizzy Holloway."

She looked us up and down before answering. I'm sure Lizzy's appearance as a Mud Monster gave her pause. When curiosity won out, she introduced herself. "I'm Evelyn McInerny, originally of the Anchor Harbor McInerny's, but call me Effie," and invited us across the street.

"Thanks so much, Effie. Pleased to meet you," I said, offering my right hand for her to shake it.

"Oh, I don't," she paused to cough. After coughing so much I thought she'd cough up a hairball, she continued, "Excuse me. I don't shake hands. Germs, ya know." She pulled a soiled hankie out to wipe some spittle from her mouth.

Lizzy and I exchanged a look. I wasn't sure if she meant our germs or hers. Deciding it didn't really matter, I kept my smile firmly in place, and told her we understood.

"Pleased to meet you both. Er, ah, I'd invite you young ladies in, but it looks like your friend," she indicated Lizzy, "fell into one of their strange traps." She pushed up her glasses, which dwarfed her face, making her resemble an owl.

"Did you say traps?" Lizzy asked.

"Yup, yup, traps. Here, why don't we go sit at the picnic table behind my house," Effie offered. "These legs don't work quite like they used to." She led us back across the street to her own faux log cabin-slash-mini-mansion.

"Nice place," Lizzy commented. I concurred.

Effie offered us some lemonade and cookies. Then proceeded to hack up the rest of that hairball on her way into the house to get our refreshments.

Once she was out of earshot, Lizzy whispered, "Let's get out of here! My skin is starting to itch. And I do not want to eat coughed-on cookies!"

"But this is a great opportunity!"

"How can it be a great opportunity? She doesn't even know who lives there!"

"But we haven't found out if she's ever heard of Marcos or that mysterious blonde woman. Or Harry, really, for that matter."

Lizzy peeled mud off her face while she thought. Glumly, she finally conceded. We sat in silence until Effie reappeared with a tray filled with glasses of lemonade and a plate of cookies. Dutifully, Lizzy and I thanked her, and took one cookie apiece.

"So now, what did you want to know again?"

I dove in, "Do you know a man named Marcos Landrostassis?"

Effie took a sip of her lemonade as she thought for a minute. "Can't say that I have. What does he do?"

"He's a sort of jack-of-all-trades from what I can gather."

"You mean, you don't know him either?"

"Well, kind of, but I've never met him face-to-face."

"Oh, I get it now. You met him on one of those interweb hootchie sites and now you're stalkin' him, eh?"

"What? No, it isn't like that at all." In a desperate need

for help, I looked at Lizzy for reinforcements.

She jumped in immediately. "Ah, what my friend is trying to say is, she is a famous writer. And she is writing a book on Marcos."

"But she hasn't met him? How can she write a book about him?" Effie had us there.

"Yes, I realize that does seem odd. I thought it was odd at first too." Lizzy gave a brief shake of her head to let me know that wasn't true. "But in this day and age, so much can be done by phone and internet. Anyway, Annie is writing a book on Marcos and is having trouble reaching him." I looked in awe at Lizzy as she just plunged right in. "She was given the address across the street as a possible place he might be."

"Doesn't she have his address?"

I thought I should speak up at this point, "No, the terms of his contract were that everything would be done remotely, er, by phone. However, he did want me to come up to the area to capture the flavor of where he lived. He was covering all of my expenses, so you can see where I'd want to do a great job for him. Only now I can't seem to find him via phone."

"Seems like a bad business all the way around."

I mumbled, "You don't even know the half of it."

"What was that, dear? My hearing is getting bad."

"Nothing, nothing. I just need to find Marcos and was hoping that the address I did get would lead me to him. What have you noticed at the house?"

"As I said, a lot of odd comings and goings, with most people wearing head-to-toe black for some reason."

"You had said something about a blonde woman, too? Have you seen a blonde woman?"

"Oh, most definitely. She comes by about every other day."

"Have you noticed anything unusual about her appearance?"

"Let me see... she always shows up at about nine

o'clock in the morning and stays about an hour. When she gets here, she has a large briefcase, but she seems to carry it lower when she leaves. Know what I mean?"

"I'm sorry I don't follow."

Lizzy asked, "Do you mean that the bag is a bit closer to the ground when she leaves? Like, maybe it's full of something?"

"Yes! That's exactly what I mean. Despite falling into one of those traps, you are a smart cookie."

Lizzy beamed at this praise. I smiled expectantly at Effie, waiting for her kind words to me. In turn, Effie sized me up, saying, "you, I'm not so sure about yet. How did you even get into this mess?"

Sigh. I bristled a bit at her commentary. But she had a point.

"I will add this, one of the men who comes by has a real scowl on his face most of the time. He has dark hair and olive skin, and when he barks out orders to the others, they listen. I just wish I knew what he was sayin'." Effie shook her head in frustration.

"Oh, is he too far away for you to hear?"

"No, he shouts really loud. That's not the problem. It's that he's speaking in another language. Greek maybe? Or Turkish? I don't know anything but English, myself."

At the mention of "Greek," Lizzy poked my leg with her foot.

"Anyway, I can't really tell you much more. That fella, he scowled a lot and that doesn't invite confidences. I'm not shy, but I'm not going where angels fear to tread."

Lizzy looked astonished. "You think he is as bad as that?"

Effie chuckled a little, perhaps at our naiveté. "I don't really know what to think, do I? I mean, it's just a saying. But there is a reason why he was creating traps, right?"

"True. Annie, my itching is getting worse. I think the mud is hardening."

"So, tell me the truth, are you girls detectives or

something?" Effie asked with a twinkle in her eye. I could tell this little visit had made her day. We had probably given her something to talk about for a few weeks.

I gently reminded her about my ghostwriting book, but I don't think she believed me. Or put another way, she chose to not believe.

Before we left, I asked her to please call me at the Lighthouse Inn if she remembered anything else. I told her to just ask for Annie.

At a mention of the Lighthouse Inn, she gave me a curious look. "You know, I think I have just person you should talk to. She's my neighbor, but she's also good friends with Millicent down at the Lighthouse Inn."

Weakly, I said, "Oh great." Next to me, I heard Lizzy groan.

"Her name is Joyce Limburger."

"Like the cheese?"

"She'll be more cooperative if you don't mention that. I'll tell her to give you a call. I'd send you over to her place now," she pointed to the yard next door to hers, "but she's gone out of town today."

"Thanks so much for your help, Effie," I said.

Lizzy was too busy trying to not itch to do more than wave as we made our way back to her Honda.

CHAPTER 13

AFTER LIZZY DROPPED ME OFF, I was too keyed up to settle down in my room. I decided to go for a drive up the scenic highway and visit Roses Rock. I was curious about going to the tip of Door County and the weather was pretty good for autumn in Wisconsin. I reached the jetty at Roses Rock in the late afternoon, just as dusk was starting. I left my car in the parking lot and took a walk around the neighborhood abutting the harbor. The air felt so lovely and free up here. I could really see settling up in Door County.

On the way back to the Lighthouse Inn, I stopped at a couple of souvenir stores. I wanted to get something to send home to Aunt Helen.

At the last shop before I headed back, I felt the hairs on the back of my neck stand up. While I pretended fascination with the contents of a Cherry Chutney jar, I cast furtive glances up and down the aisle. Slowly and subtly, I turned around, but couldn't see anyone.

I put down the chutney, and walked to the cashier. Hoping I wasn't becoming paranoid with all of the odd goings-on lately, I convinced myself I was imagining things.

The cashier had her head down, cleaning her area before close. With her long red hair hanging in her face, it was tough making eye contact.

"Hey!" I greeted her. Her name tag said Beth.

She looked up, startled. Pushing up glasses that were clearly too big for her painfully thin face. "Oh hey, I hadn't realized someone was in here with me."

So much for gleaning any observations from her. And apparently, she wasn't cleaning, but playing a game on her phone. However, desperate times, and you know the rest.

Feeling like I needed to talk fast to keep her tentative attention, I dove in. "Did you happen to see someone else in the store?" Good luck to me, since she didn't even see me.

"I didn't see anyone el—" She was cut off by the storeroom door slamming shut and a glass jar breaking. Before we could get to the back of the store, the person was gone.

"Beth, you go down that aisle!" I directed her to the aisle to my left. Her lanky limbs took off like a shot. I sprinted down another aisle and we met back by the register.

"How did you know my name anyway?" Beth narrowed her eyes.

A bit winded from the sprint, I pointed at her name tag. Her eyes narrowed more, then she looked at where I was pointing and realized. Smacking her hand on her forehead, she giggled.

"Yeah, I always forget about that. Most days I forget to even put it on. Who are you anyway?"

Able to breathe and talk again, I told her my name and we shook hands.

"So, is someone following you? How cool is that!" Beth exclaimed. "Nothing exciting ever happens around here!" Suddenly, we heard a crash that sounded like it came from the storeroom area. Running back down the aisles, we saw a black work boot as it tore out of a side door I hadn't noticed before.

"Is this side door one that's usually open?" I looked over at Beth. We heard a Harley rev up and peel out of the lot.

Looking a bit pale, she nodded. "But no one ever uses it. We just use it for deliveries. It goes straight out to the side parking lot, which we share with that fish boil place next door." *Oh, fish boils—how fun! Ok, wait, focus!* Was I being followed? What seemed so out of the ordinary now seemed quite ordinary. Shaken, I headed back to my car and tentatively turned it on. Closing my eyes as the ignition sparked, I let out a relieved sigh that a car bomb didn't go. *Silly.* I shook my head at my dramatic behavior. A car bomb. *Honestly, what would I think of next?*

Although the sky had started to darken, the rain held off long enough for me to view a gorgeous sunset before I began to head back. It was impossible to enjoy it, given my rising nervousness. Realizing someone might be following me gave me jitters. The rain beat down on my windshield, seeming to keep time with my pounding heart. As a result, I took my time driving back to the Lighthouse Inn (even though I wanted to speed back). I drove down Highway 42, passing a few cars here and there. When a deer bounded across the highway, I tried to apply my brakes. Missing the deer by inches, my panic only increased because my brakes didn't take. *What the heck? Is this it? This is how it ends.* The last few days passed in front of my eyes.

I tried to pump the brakes. No good. Nothing. I didn't even slow down. I heard screaming in the car as I careened down the highway, then screamed more when I realized it was me.

In my panicked haze, I tried to remember what grandpa told me to do.

"Annie, you need to turn into it." No, no, that was how to avoid ice patches.

"Put a little dirt on it." Nope, that wasn't even driving.

Why couldn't I remember? Maybe I should stop

screaming and take a deep breath. *Calm down, Annie. You can do this*. I seemed to be slowing down. Again, I put my foot all the way down on the brake.

Suddenly, I remembered everything grandpa had shared with me. I tried my emergency brake, which slowed me down a little. When I got down to 10 miles per hour and the road started to slope uphill, I decided to turn into something soft to stop moving. Just ahead, I saw my mark. I prayed that this maneuver would work. I grabbed my steering wheel and made turn onto the shoulder. My car started to slow down a little as I hit foliage.

Crashing into a thick hedge caused a huge splash of twigs and crisp leaves. My car skidded a little bit more and came to a stop. I caught my breath.

I heard knocking on my window. Dazed, I looked up. I felt really fuzzy. The knocking continued. Someone called my name.

"Annie? Annie, open up!"

Confused, I squinted out the window through the rain. I saw a vaguely familiar face looking at me.

Donovan? What was he doing here?

I opened my door.

"Are you okay? Do you need help?"

"I think my brakes went out," I said. I had known I needed new brakes. That seemed like the understatement of the year. I sat there for a minute, trying to register what had happened. "But with the rain and everything, I'm not really sure."

"But you're okay, right? No broken bones?" I nodded that I was fine. He got out his phone and made a phone call.

He snapped his phone shut. "I just called a tow truck for you. They'll be here in about 20 minutes."

"Thanks a bunch. What are you doing here anyway?"

"I had just turned onto the highway and saw you lose control of your car. I thought I should probably help whoever was in the car."

"I really appreciate your help. It's kind of funny, I keep bumping into you in odd ways."

He smiled down at me. "Lucky for me. I never did get your number. You practically flew out of my car at the police station."

"Oh, you wanted my number?" I looked down to hide my blushing. I couldn't seem to do anything but blush around this guy.

"I was hoping for it. But I understand if you don't want to give it to a strange guy whose nose you broke."

"I didn't break your nose," I began indignantly. When I saw his smile, I gave a little laugh, "you got me again. I think we can work something out." I smiled and looked up at him. "In the meantime, do you think we need to call the cops about my car?"

"I don't think so. You hit the hedge, but it looks improved by the impact. Nope, I think the tow truck will be enough."

I pulled out my cell phone to see the time. My grandfather had called a few times, and I kept missing his calls because of the spotty coverage up here. I really needed to change my cell phone carrier. With the storm raging over us, Donovan invited me to sit in his car while we waited for the tow truck. Whenever Donovan looked at me, he smiled. I started to feel self-conscious and grew bright red. I felt my ears get warm, which made me feel even more shy. Sigh, I felt ridiculous being twenty-two and still getting so nervous around someone I liked, but I didn't have a lot of experience with guys. Grandpa had been rather overprotective because of what my Mom had been through.

"Seriously, how is it that I keep bumping into you?"

"Door County isn't that big. I'm sure you've seen the same people a few times a day up here. I've even heard theories of a similar phenomenon before. It goes something like this. Before you meet someone, you probably have seen them before, up to two or three

111

times."

"What do you mean? Like a face in the crowd?" I scrunched up my nose.

"Exactly like that. Only we (you and I) have become conscious of our face in the crowd moments, which makes it feel like I'm stalking you." At this comment, we both laughed. Despite my weird day, I felt myself relaxing.

"Annie, do you need a ride home? I am at your service."

"Well, um… yeah, I think I'll need to take you up on that offer. I hope it isn't too much trouble."

"Nope, none at all."

"I really appreciate this. I could've waited for a cab, but I'm not even sure that's possible up here, is it?"

"Yeah, no, not so much. Hey, how did your interrogation go the other day?"

"Other than being told I couldn't leave town, it went okay." I hesitated telling Donovan more. On one hand, I felt comfortable with him; on the other hand, I really didn't know him very well.

"Don't worry about that. That's standard operating procedure. Did the detective treat you all right?"

"For the most part he did. He was kind of a hard nose, but I guess he has a reputation of being very by the book. He asked me how I knew Marcos Landrostassis, which I thought was kind of odd at the time. But now I can't get in touch with Marcos, so I'm really confused about it all."

"Considering that your project was about Marcos, that doesn't seem too odd that he asked you about him. Really. I wouldn't worry if I were you. Just remember, Chad Dupah tends to be really thorough." Donovan kept his eyes on the road as we spoke and didn't notice my sharp glance at him. How on earth did he know it was Chad who had interviewed me? Sigh. Yet one more mystery.

Shrugging off my concerns, I tried to change the subject, "You know where I live. Where do you live?"

"I have a little place in Michigan City. And when I'm

not being an insurance agent, I'm a superhero who rescues beautiful women who drive into hedges." He made a flourishing bow, and I laughed. Well, whoever he was, he was certainly charming.

The tow truck came and did what they do best—my car got towed. I had already gotten my purse out of the car. I gave the tow truck guy my information, and he promised to keep me updated. I thanked him, and he drove off. Donovan and I got into his blue Jeep and made our way down Highway 42.

We sat outside the inn for a minute. "After coming to my rescue and everything, why don't you come in for a drink? My treat."

"I'd love to." We got out of his car and made our way into the Lighthouse. Kitty had a couple of bartenders at the Lighthouse, Lizzy and a guy named George. Since Lizzy had the night off, George had the bar all to himself. Although I didn't know George well, he always seemed affable and not easily flustered, which are great qualities for a bartender.

"What'll you have?" George asked, almost the minute we sat. I gave him my order of a glass of red wine and looked at Donovan for his order. Donovan decided on their Oktoberfest selection from the microbrewery. I put a ten out on the bar for George to collect. Donovan took the ten and gave it back to me.

"This one is on me." He dropped his money on the bar. "So, tell me more about this book," Donovan said.

"I don't really know what more there is to tell. I think I covered most of it already. Harry's company… well really, Harry… contacted me to ghostwrite a book about Marcos Landrostassis. Only now Harry's dead and I think I'm a possible suspect. Plus, I can't seem to find Marcos." At that moment, George brought our drinks.

I shrugged. "I mean, most of it is in the notes I made. The kind of notes that most writers make when working on a book. I took down Marcos' story while he gave a running narrative."

"Is there anything in particular that stood out in his story? Any odd behavior?"

"Other than the niggling feeling I had that he might be insane? No, nothing I can think of."

Donovan lifted his glass and gestured for me to do the same. "Well, then I propose a toast to the resolution of this matter."

"I can drink to that!" I said heartily as we clinked glasses. "You know, I feel uncommonly comfortable with you. I don't know why."

"Yeah, ditto with you. It should be noted, too, that I don't normally feel this comfortable with someone I just met." He took a long drink of his beer.

I blushed. Again. Grr... when would I get out of middle school for goodness' sake?

"So, um, any chance for me to come up and see your manuscript?"

If possible, I turned more red. What do I do in this situation? I hadn't dated that much. And, I definitely wasn't the type to have a one-night stand.

The panic must have reflected in my eyes because Donovan grabbed my hand and said, "Whoa, whoa, we don't have to do anything you are uncomfortable with. I like you, Annie. And I really would like to see your manuscript. I'd like to learn more about you."

I gave him a tremulous smile and nodded. He moved in closer, leaning in as he looked at my mouth. Just when something exciting was about to happen which would turn into me giving him the green light to see my manuscript, his phone rang.

Donovan looked at his display briefly. "I do have to take this. Please excuse me." He quickly walked towards the hallway.

I barely had time to take another sip of wine before Donovan rushed back to the bar. He grabbed his jacket and said hurriedly, "I'm so sorry, I'll have to take a rain check on seeing your manuscript. Something urgent just came up. I'll talk to you soon, though." And with that, he left the room.

I shrugged. I had no idea what his emergency was. I certainly hoped it wasn't another woman, but I didn't know him well. It very well could be. I mean, I know insurance agents have to deal with emergencies to some degree, but he left very hurriedly. After pondering it for a few more minutes, I opted to take my wine up to my room, order room service for dinner, and read a bit before bed.

•••

The next morning, I opted to call Grandpa first. Since our last call had ended a bit abruptly, I wanted to find out how Aunt Helen was doing. Despite what they thought, it wasn't my goal to worry him and Aunt Helen.

I punched in Grandpa's number and waited. Both he and Aunt Helen were hard of hearing, and they didn't always hear the phone. In the past, I had already counted up to ten rings waiting for them to answer.

"Hello, Frank here," said Grandpa.

"Hiya Papa," I tried to inject a light tone in my voice.

"Don't you 'hiya' me, Annie Malone. We have been worried sick over you."

"Worried, why?" I mean, if they knew about the last 24 hours, I knew they'd be worried, but they didn't. So, I didn't understand why they were worried sick.

"So, you really found a dead body the other day?"

"I did. Has the news been all over it down there?"

"Bits and pieces, but we haven't seen your name on the news yet. Have you been interviewed at all?"

"No, the press hasn't gotten ahold of me yet." Pausing a little on the word press, I hoped Grandpa didn't notice.

Grandpa groaned. "I'm not talking about the press. I'm talking about the cops." He could always tell when I was trying to hide something. Of course, with my expressive voice and his time as a detective, I shouldn't be shocked that he found me out.

"I may have had to give a statement. But that's pretty standard, right?"

"For the most part, yes. But I sense something's up. All right, Annie, what the hell is going on?"

"Grandpa, seriously, I don't know. I took this writing job and I found a dead guy. You know as much as I do."

"I have a half a mind to make you move back home. You know, you aren't too old for me to take you over my knee." Grandpa pulled out the old standards whenever he was scared for me. Fortunately, he couldn't see my epic eye roll over the phone. I thought, at twenty-two years old, I probably was too old to be pulled over his knee. However, respect for his age and position prevented me for saying it.

"I'm okay, Grandpa. I'll be fine. I'll call you once I know more."

"You'd better. Stay safe, Anna Banana."

We hung up.

Before I even put down the phone, Donovan called me.

"Hello?" I said.

"Hi! How are you feeling?"

"Much better, thanks. Thanks again for slaying my dragons yesterday."

"Yeah, we need to talk about that." Uh, okay, so that's how it's going to be. I guess he was expecting the payback now. I should have known he was too good to be true. I knew something had seemed off-kilter with him.

"Oh?"

"Can you meet me downstairs at noon? Lunch is on me."

"Now you sound mysterious."

"I don't mean to. Just trust me on this."

"Oh great. Whenever a guy says, 'trust me,' it means

the exact opposite."

I heard his smile over the phone. "All right, ya got me. I'm going to kidnap you in the middle of the lunch crowd and take you to my secret lair in the Peninsula State Park."

"You have a secret lair? I'm impressed. Okay, sorry for the paranoia. I'll be there."

I ended the call. Despite losing my job, finding a dead body, and having my brakes fail on me, I felt pretty good.

CHAPTER 14

TOO BAD THAT GOOD FEELING DIDN'T last. I stared at Donovan open-mouthed.

We were sitting in Dublin's pub, which really did have the best salmon sandwiches in the world (Janie might have even undersold them). I had ordered one of these yummy sandwiches and a lovely pint of Strongbow cider. Donovan had a Guinness and a club sandwich in front of him. Sitting there, having lunch with Donovan felt like most normal thing in the world, and I hadn't had normal in a few days. When Donovan had asked me to meet him downstairs, I had assumed he'd meant that we'd eat at the Lighthouse Inn. Turns out he meant that he'd pick me up downstairs and whisk me away to Turtle Bay.

"What did you just say?" I put down my sandwich.

"I said, 'I'm not who you think I am,'" he repeated himself.

"Well, really who among us is?" I laughed, trying to lighten the suddenly oppressive mood. So, what was he saying? That he had a long-lost insane wife he had committed to living in his attic? A sister who had eloped with an inappropriate suitor at 16 years old? An uncle who sent ships to their demise with his band of wreckers?

Okay, okay I shouldn't let my imagination get the best of me as I went through the plots of some of my favorite books. Of course, based on the events of the last few days, I felt that anything was possible.

"I'm serious, I haven't been completely frank with you." He made as if he was going to reach for my hand, but then seemed to think better of it.

"And I don't know how to tell you because I find myself very attracted to you." He looked deeply into my eyes and said, "I need to tell you th-…"

"Excuse me, sir, are you Donovan Archer?" the waitress approached the table. "There is an urgent call for you at the hostess stand."

He cringed for a split-second. "Okay. Thanks." As he made his way up, he squeezed my shoulder briefly. "I'll explain everything when I come back."

I was starting to feel a bit nauseous. The feeling of normalcy was riding off into the sunset and eating my salmon sandwich. My appetite was quickly leaving me.

I blinked a few times. He was taking another call now? In the middle of our conversation. The hostess did say it was urgent. But why didn't whoever it was try to call his cell phone if it was that urgent? Out of the corner of my eye, I spied his cell phone sitting on the table. Would you look at that? He left his cell phone just sitting there, begging to be picked up. Hmmm… while I was ordinarily not a nosy person, I was in an extraordinary situation, which called for extraordinary actions. Right?

So, before I could even control myself, I eagerly grabbed his phone to see his contact list. My ears burned and I dropped it like a hot potato. I did catch a glimpse of an incoming text with a non-local area code.

From across the room, I saw Donovan head back to our table and guiltily looked down. A slight flush covered my face. I drank some of my water to calm down.

"Sorry about that. I really don't like taking calls in restaurants, but I had let my client know to call me here if

119

anything urgent came up."

"An insurance emergency? Sure, that makes sense. I certainly had one yesterday, right?" I still wasn't getting it.

"Yes. Exactly. Well, not exactly." Donovan rubbed his neck and avoided eye contact.

"I'm sorry, I'm not following." I took a huge drink of my Strongbow cider. I had a feeling I'd need it.

"It's part of what I wanted to tell you."

"You know what, I've dealt with a lot in the past few days and this sandwich is really good. Can I finish it and then we'll talk?"

Donovan smiled indulgently at me, "Sure, that's not a problem." Again, he made like he wanted to hold my hand across the table, then stopped himself.

Sighing, I recalled when I used to have conversations with people, and the conversations made sense. Now, I felt like Alice down the rabbit hole. Every day. Not a pleasant experience.

When we finished our meal, Donovan signaled that the waitress bring our bill immediately. "Do you mind if we head over to the bar to talk?" Donovan asked once he paid the bill.

"Why?"

"I'd like a better view of the whole restaurant."

"Um, sure, okay," and so we meandered over the bar. Donovan sat on the barstool closest to the far wall and kept looking at the door like he expected someone any minute. What was going on?

He ordered a Strongbow for me and a Guinness for himself.

"Actually, I could use something stronger," I muttered.

He called the bartender back over and ordered two shots of rye whiskey also. The bartender brought the shots over first and they were gone by the time he brought the pints.

Donovan must have sensed some of the tension ebb from me. He asked me if I was ready to talk. I told him I was.

"I'm a private investigator. I wasn't supposed to tell you because I was tailing you for my client. But now I have a different task and you need to know who I really am." He took a long drink of his Guinness.

"You've been what? You're a what?" I looked around to see if I was being pranked by someone. "What do I call you now?"

This? On top of everything else? Really, a PI?

"Donovan. Same as before."

"And what do you do?"

"As a private investigator? Some security work. Quite a bit of work in Green Bay, actually. Usually, my work is for insurance agencies, but this case is a bit different. And I'm doing a special favor for an old Army buddy. Last night, when I wanted to see your manuscript…"

"…and notes," I added.

"Yes, and notes, my interest in their ongoing activities was the real reason I wanted to see them, but I couldn't tell you."

"In case you had to kill me?" I joked, inappropriately trying to make light of the situation because of my nervousness.

"No, in case you had killed Harry. But, as I said, my assignment has changed."

I gulped. "Oh."

"I'm so sorry. Were you close to Harry?"

"Not really. But he was my editor, so there was a certain familiarity." I sipped my drink slowly, taking in this newest information.

A curious thought struck me. It occurred to me that it was a pretty big coincidence that I met Donovan while I was working on Marcos' book. I couldn't ignore the wire-tapping implications. I mean, how else would he have known to tail me, of all people, right?

"No, I wasn't tapping your phone. I'm not the FBI," he answered my unspoken question. "My client got the information from Marcos' phone."

"Is Marcos that big of a deal? I mean I know he's been implicated in petty crimes, but that doesn't seem like enough to warrant all of this fuss about him."

"We think so. We suspect that the petty crimes might be a smokescreen for some of the bigger stuff he's involved in. I can't go into more detail, but we are trying to catch up with whoever is controlling the whole operation."

"Okay, that's all well and good, but why were you following me? I realize now that you hadn't just succumbed to my charms. I realize that I was under surveillance. Why?"

He had the grace to blush at this statement.

"At first, I was only monitoring you." Here, he made a weird, catching noise with his throat.

"Ahem, that is to say, until you went after me at that store," he said.

"You started liking me because I made a public scene?"

"When our eyes met at the store, I knew I had to meet you. You might be a bit shy, but you are a firecracker when you let loose."

"Seriously? That's how you're going to play this now?"

"Play this? What do you mean? I just paid you a compliment."

That I couldn't deny, but I still didn't trust him. "You were tailing me because of your job, and you happened to think I was cute. Big deal." The whiskey made me a little sassy, but it had to be said. I could not be sucked into this weird, unknown area. I needed to really stay focused on keeping this relationship clearly professional now that I knew most of the story. Er, of course, I was assuming I knew most of the story. That assumption would almost cost me everything.

"Okay. Okay. So sue me, I thought, and still do think, that you were cute. You are cute. Hell, your curls are enough to drive me mad. And I could get lost in the depths of your eyes. But I can't do anything about it," he said.

I felt a twinge of disappointment, "Why not?"

"Because you are now under my protection, and I need to keep my distance, ironically."

"I'm under your protection? How do you figure? I mean, I know you helped me out when my brakes failed, but protection? Isn't that a bit much?"

"Your brakes didn't fail. Your brake line was cut."

At this, I fell off the barstool and fainted in a heap on the floor.

CHAPTER 15

"**A**NNIE? CAN YOU HEAR ME?"

"Er, miss?"

"Hey, her eyes are fluttering open."

I coughed. Someone had put some whiskey on my upper lip. I had a splitting headache and was looking at the ceiling of the bar at Dublin's. I didn't think I had drunk that much. I looked at the faces around me. I saw several faces I didn't recognize—no surprise there. Then I saw Donovan, and it all came flooding back to me. I held my throbbing head.

"Here, Annie, lemme help you up." Donovan gingerly grabbed me under the arms and guided me to one of the regular chairs in the alcove near the bar area. "There you go, have a seat." Fortunately, the lunch crowd had left, and the bar was empty.

He handed me a glass of water. "Drink it up. It should help." I did as ordered. "There you go." I couldn't read the look he gave me.

I dribbled some on my chin. Embarrassed, I wiped it away and wouldn't look at him. The memory of our conversation came flooding back to me.

He grabbed my chin and made me look at him.

"What do you mean, my brake line was cut?" I asked, much more timidly than I felt. Stupid fainting spell. I seemed to faint at exactly the wrong time. Once, I fainted at the sight of my own blood, from a very small cut. I was only out for a few seconds, but when I came to, a fuse in the house had blown, which really confused me for a minute.

"I can't divulge that right now. But I didn't mean to make you faint in a heap like that."

I interrupted him, "I didn't fall in a heap. I *swooned* with dignity, like a lady."

"Sure, if that's how you want it. I'm sorry, but the LEOs (law enforcement officers to you) involved had to impound your car until further notice."

What the what? I groaned. *No car. No job. Involved in a murder, or whatever, investigation. What next?* I groaned again. My head really hurt.

"When do I get my car back? I need to start looking for work soon." Very soon. "My latest project seems to have developed a huge glitch."

"Well, here's the thing, you aren't safe right now. And you can't really leave town. Besides, you can't have your car back until we figure out who cut the line. I need you to keep a lower profile, okay?"

I held my head and groaned again, nodding slightly. I really hoped the one-man band would stop drumming in my head.

"Did Harry know something?" I asked, already knowing the answer. He must have known something, or figured out something. Harry knowing something certainly explained his odd behavior during our last phone call. I thought about his mad dash up to Door County and taking me off the project, too. Was it possible he was trying to protect me?

"We think that Harry knew something, based on the way he was killed. We think they think you know the same thing."

"I don't think I know anything. I mean, Marcos shared a lot of information with me, but all of it was pertaining to his insistence of innocence, and, as you pointed out, more aligned with his petty crimes. However, I think you're right about Harry. He seemed to want to tell me something. He also said something about feeling badly that he had put me in danger."

"I think he was right; you really are in danger. And probably should leave the Lighthouse for a while. You and Lizzy Holloway have become good friends, right? Would you be able to move in with her and her family until this whole thing blows over? They don't live too far from here, and I'm sure they'd welcome you. If you go stay with them, I could investigate further, and I'd know you were safe."

My head shot up, "What? Are you kidding me?"

"Look, you're being watched by Marcos or his goons." At this, I started to laugh hysterically. The shock of the last 24 hours was setting in.

Donovan eyed me warily. "What's so funny?" he asked tentatively.

"Nothing, really. None of this is funny," I said, gasping to catch my breath. "It's just that I had gotten upset with Marcos during one of our interviews and called him a big goon."

"Yeah, well, I guess you weren't too far off, huh?" He cracked a little smile.

•••

After Donovan and I had finished up at Dublin's pub in Turtle Bay, I was still determined to not move from the Lighthouse Inn. Kitty had been so kind to me, and I really adored my independence. Since I had promised to give another statement regarding my brakes and whatnot, Donovan drove me to the police station in Michigan City right after our surreal lunch. I still liked him down deep, but I was upset that he had lied about his identity. Plus, I was consumed with confusion. Then he dropped me off at the Lighthouse. I decided to take a nap and fell into a fitful sleep and had a very weird dream.

In my dream, I was in a strange home that I didn't recognize. A faceless man appeared and chased me out of his house into the dark night. The faceless man turned into Harry, who then warned me, "Beware of the **redhead**."

Suddenly, Donovan ran to my side and we were back in my old apartment. He held me close.

"It's okay. Don't worry. We'll solve this." I nestled in, he smelled good. He lifted my chin. He kissed me softly. His lips touching mine felt really good. I put my arms around him.

Suddenly, my cell phone rang. Somewhere in my hazy mind, I heard the phone ringing and wondered why it kept ringing. But the kiss felt so good. I was beginning to really appreciate Donovan's qualities.

He, on the other hand, had the instincts of a cop and pushed me away. He ran to the living room to get my phone, which had become a banana. When he turned around to bring the phone back to me, he knocked into me and dropped my still-ringing banana. We both went to pick it up and knocked heads a la the Three Stooges.

"Ouch," I cried out.

"Oh, I'm so sorry," he said as he quickly recovered his wits and bent again to grab the banana.

"No, no it's okay. I'm sorry." He smiled as he handed me the banana. It had already stopped ringing, and we just stood, looking stupidly at each other with big dopey grins.

My banana rang again, this time in my hands. The ringing startled me and I almost dropped it again. I checked the display: 999-9999. Creepy.

Wordlessly, Donovan urged me to answer it.

"Hello?"

"Are you Annie?" a synthesized voice asked me. The voice sounded like a machine talking, very robotic.

"Y-yes, I-I am. What do you want?"

"Here's to your s-s-s-silence." Ew, that sounded like a hiss, like a snake. Gross and super-creepy. I heard a clinking sound in the background, like a glass being toasted. "Do you like the present we left for you?"

"Present? What present?" I looked up at Donovan, who shrugged and motioned for the phone. Quietly, I held up the phone for Donovan to listen, too.

"We so carefully hid it. We hope you find it in time."

I whispered to him, "Should we look for this present? Do you think it's a clue or another warning?"

Donovan shot me a look of alarm. He flipped my banana shut and told me to leave now. He threw the banana into the linen closet and shut the door. I looked at him, quizzically.

"Now?"

"Grab your jacket. Nothing else! We are leaving now!" he ordered.

As we shut my apartment door and raced down the stairs, I felt my breath leave me as we heard an explosion. I felt heat at my back. I was too scared to turn around.

Even though the banana had exploded, I could still hear a phone ringing. Ring. Ring. The sound cut through the haze of my dream. Cautiously, I opened one eye and looked around my room at the Lighthouse. Whew! Everything looked intact. Nothing looked blown up. I let out a huge sigh of relief. I looked at my phone (which hadn't become a banana) to see who had just called. Grandpa. Still shaken by my vivid dream, I figured I'd wait a bit to call him back.

Naturally, that dream really stunned me, but it was just a dream, right? Heck, I had had wild dreams before. No biggie.

But the next day, someone broke into my room and had their way with it. And that was a big deal.

CHAPTER 16

THE FOLLOWING NIGHT, I HUNG OUT at the Lighthouse bar while Lizzy worked. I needed to be around people and was able to read my book in between chatting with Lizzy and others. A couple of times, I thought I saw Donovan enter the bar. And, as welcome as seeing him would have been on one level, I was still a bit annoyed with his highhandedness. When Lizzy and I got to my room to brainstorm about the case after her shift, it must have been around ten-ish. We couldn't help but notice that my door was slightly ajar. I knew that I had shut and locked the door. Growing up in Milwaukee made locking doors second nature to me. Even the air felt different. I would have sworn I smelled the hint of cigarette smoke in my room. This was odd since I didn't smoke, and I knew that the Lighthouse Inn had a strict "No Smoking" policy.

I staggered back from the door, afraid to even touch the knob.

"What's wrong, Annie?" asked Lizzy. She had been a few steps behind me. Almost immediately after she asked the question, she saw my open door. "Annie, why is your door open? Didn't you shut it?"

"Of course!" I didn't know what to do with my hands. They wouldn't stop shaking.

Lizzy entered the room slowly, pushing past me. "Hello? Hello?"

"Lizzy? Why are you greeting a burglar?"

"Maybe it isn't a burglar. Maybe someone got really cold and decided that your room looked warm and inviting."

I looked at her in shock. I'll admit, her argument went far to take my mind off of what had happened.

"Well, in any case, Annie, someone did break into your room. I think we should do a sweep of the room." Lizzy checked the closet and bathroom, and even looked under the bed. Still in shock, I slowly made my way around the room, which had been tossed like a salad. I looked at her rather stupidly, not sure what to say. As the fog lifted, I noticed that all of the drawers had been pulled out. My laptop had been moved from the desk to the coffee table. But it was still there. Also, in addition to the couch cushions being upturned, the bed was a mess and my luggage was open, with the lining ripped out.

"Focus, Annie. You need to stay calm. Why would anyone do this? I don't want to alarm you…" Lizzy said, walking over to the desk.

"Too late."

"I've seen enough crime shows to know that whoever did this was looking for something. Do you have any idea what that might be?"

"No. I don't have anything worth taking." I sank down onto the bed with head in my hands.

"Well, someone thinks you do." With her arm, Lizzy gestured towards the mess in my room.

"What do I do now?" I asked, "Call the cops?" I stood up and began to pace around the room.

"Probably, yeah," Lizzy began. "That wou-… oops!"

One of the few things left untouched was the mug from Harry. Which Lizzy had just knocked off the desk. It broke apart into a million white pieces dotted with colored pieces of glass. Wait, colored pieces of glass? That's odd. The mug itself had been really plain, just white stoneware with Harry's logo in black on the side.

Lizzy looked at me, then back down at the mug. "Oh my gosh! Look, Annie! Do you see that?"

Why was she making such a big deal about a broken mug? Had she forgotten that someone had broken into my room?

"Oh, don't worry about it, Lizzy," I said. "Seriously, the mug is no big deal. I mean, I would just like to know who killed Harry and, now, who trashed my room. But it's easy to clean up some stoneware and bits of glass." I started to go into the hallway to get the dustpan from the utility closet (Kitty had shown me where it was kept earlier that day).

"Wait!" Lizzy yelled to me. I stopped. She continued, "Look more closely at those colored glass pieces on the floor. Doesn't it seem odd that a black and white mug would have colored pieces of glass mixed in with its shards?"

At Lizzy's question, I turned around and looked at her.

She tried to quirk her eyebrow. "Just take a look at the colored pieces of glass on the floor, okay? Tell me what you see."

Shrugging, I complied. Being careful to avoid little shards of mug, I got down on my hands and knees to view the glass pieces more closely.

Ruby red, emerald green, sapphire blue, and diamond sparkly colors made themselves apparent. My mouth dropped open. Wide-eyed, I looked up at Lizzy. She realized I finally understood and nodded knowingly at me.

"Gems?" I squeaked out.

"Gems. From the looks of it, you have a King's ransom sitting here."

"What's next with this? This puts a whole new angle on why Harry was killed, doesn't it?"

"I think it narrows things down. Especially since now we can assume his murder probably wasn't random."

"I think I'm gonna be sick."

Lizzy looked over at me, alarmed. She crossed the room to my side and put an arm around me, "Steady. Try to stay calm."

"Stay calm? In the past week and a half, I have quit my job, moved away from home, been screamed at by my client, found my editor dead, had my room ransacked, found out the guy I like is an FBI agent who was investigating me, and discovered jewels—probably stolen jewels—hidden in a mug." To my horror, I started to blubber, "And you are telling me to 'stay calm.' You 'stay calm!'"

"What happened?" came Kitty's voice from the doorway. She saw my stricken face and ran over to us, "What's wrong? Are you okay?"

"D-d-do I-I l-lo-o-ok o-okay?" I said between sobs. Kitty offered me a tissue and wrapped her arms around us.

"Annie's having a rough week, I think," explained Lizzy. A bit of an understatement. They both patted my shoulders. I felt like we'd like been here before.

Kitty broke the hug first and declared, "Well, first things first. We need to get this mess taken care of. Then we need to figure out what to do."

Lizzy ran to the closet to get the cleaning materials, including the dustpan. As she left the room, she called back to me, "Annie, see if Kitty can spot the stuff!"

Looking at me quizzically, Kitty said, "Stuff? What stuff?" Wordlessly, I pointed to the jumbled mess of broken mug shards and jewels.

"I'm sorry, I still don't see it. All I see are a bunch of pottery shards."

"Maybe this will help. The mug that broke was only white and black, it didn't have any color on it," I explained as I wiped my eyes and blew my nose.

Kitty ducked to get a closer look at the remains of the

mug. "What the heck? What are all these little pieces of…?"

"Colored glass?"

"Yeah."

"No. Look more closely."

"These are GEMS!"

"Yep," Lizzy said as she re-entered the room with the supplies.

"Oh my gosh! Where did they come from?"

"I don't know if you remember that stoneware mug that Harry gave me?"

Kitty screwed up her face in thought. "Nope, can't place it. But is that why your room looks like a tornado went through it?"

"Near as I can figure. We also think it may be why Harry was killed."

Kitty helped Lizzy and me clean up the mess. Our task took us until after midnight. The three of us decided to hide the jewels. Clearly, someone wanted them. I didn't want to keep them, but I did want to find out who wanted them. Kitty said she could keep them in the Lighthouse's safe.

"The Lighthouse has a safe?" Lizzy said, clearly surprised.

"All hotels do, honey. Of course we have one. Remind me to show you where it is. And, for you, Annie, I'm thinking that you should probably temporarily move to another location."

"I think you're right. Someone is clearly trying to get to me. But where should I go?"

"Let me talk to my sister and brother-in-law. I'm sure they'd let you stay with us. You can sleep in the room I'm in, it's the guest room. I don't think it will be a problem. If it's okay with both of you, I'll head home now and talk to Maggie and Nick first thing in the morning."

"Oh, would you Lizzy? Do you mind? It would really help me out. But I don't want to put your family in danger."

"Pish! We thrive on danger," Lizzy said jokingly as she wriggled her eyebrows. "But, seriously, it won't be a problem. I don't think you'll be putting us in danger. I doubt they—whoever 'they' are—will know where you've gone."

Kitty left shortly after Lizzy. Before leaving, she made sure that I was okay to sleep in the room alone. I reassured her that I'd be okay for one more night alone in the room.

She added. "Look, you are clearly in danger here. I think that you need to leave for Maggie and Nick's right away in the morning. I don't want you to go, but you do need to be in a better location." She turned to leave, then thought better of it and came back. "Also, I don't think we should tell the cops about the gems at this point. I don't think we should make it public that you found them. Can we trust that PI guy hanging around you?"

"I think so."

I turned on the TV for white noise right after Kitty shut the door. My mind kept churning over this recent development. Why were gems in the mug Harry gave me? What could that possibly mean? I assumed Harry wasn't that generous. Those jewels had to be worth a lot of money.

At about three in the morning, I woke up to my cell phone ringing. Darn it all! Only a few hours of sleep for me. The ringing crept into my dreaming subconscious. I thought my alarm was going off and that I kept getting air when I tried to hit snooze. The ringing wouldn't stop. Finally, I swam to the surface of consciousness and realized my phone was ringing. Oh my gosh, who the heck is calling at this time of the night? I wondered as I raced to my cell phone. The phone stopped ringing just as I picked it up. I saw 11 missed calls on my phone's display. All of the calls had happened between two and three. Clearly, someone wanted to contact me, but didn't want to leave a message. The missed calls also didn't display a real number, only "000-0000." I felt a deep chill go down my back. Had my dream been that prophetic? The phone rang again, startling me out of my reverie. I dropped the phone as I tried to answer it.

It rang four times before I could get it. Finally, I breathlessly answered, "Hello? Who is this?"

A synthetic voice box said, menacingly, "This is your worst nightmare. You should never have gotten involved in this. Give us the jewels and don't ever contact Marcos and Diana Landrostassis again."

"Who are you? Why are you doing this?"

"This has nothing to do with you. If you get out now, you won't suffer the same fate as Harry."

"What are you talk—," I began to say when the faceless voice abruptly hung up on me. Unable to sleep again, I decided I might as well get up and continue working on a plan of action for our informal investigation. I felt even more compelled to find Marcos.

CHAPTER 17

KITTY HAD AGREED TO CALL DONOVAN with the news of my temporary residence. I felt shy about talking to him, but given his involvement in the case, we felt he should know where I was staying. Kitty handled the cops, too. She did have a legitimate break-in, so they needed to be called. Since I had to leave a lot of my stuff behind for the cops' investigation, I only packed one small bag. Fortunately, they let me grab my laptop.

Lizzy came to pick me later that morning. Our drive to her sister's house was pretty uneventful and quiet, which helped soothe my nerves. I was still in shock about the recent events and told Lizzy about my dream and the call I had earlier that morning. Clearly shaken, Lizzy almost drove off the road when I told her about the voice on the phone.

I sunk a little lower in my seat and stayed quiet for the rest of the short drive.

I wasn't sure what to expect when I met Lizzy's sister and brother-in-law, but I was pleasantly surprised. They were even nicer than I had imagined. Since Lizzy had filled them in on the situation, they hadn't gone to work before we arrived. We got there around eight thirty a.m. and they welcomed me with open arms. Lizzy made the introductions and raced inside to get the bed ready. Well, not really a bed. Lizzy had told me that since she lived in their guest room, we'd be sharing a room. She'd keep her bed and I'd be on the couch. She had wanted me to take the bed, but I couldn't do that to her.

Her sister, Maggie Williams, hugged and fussed over me as though she'd always known me. Maggie had the same blond curly hair as Lizzy, but she wore it a little shorter. She stood a little taller than Lizzy and was almost a full foot taller than me. Her husband, Nick Williams, was a big guy, probably as tall as Donovan, but with an extra 30 pounds. Dressed in jeans and a sweater, Maggie was taking the day off from her job as a kindergarten teacher. Nick was also dressed in jeans and had arranged to work from home that day.

When Kitty made the arrangements with Donovan, she arranged for him to meet us there. He arrived soon after we did and called out to Nick so they could talk. I heard Donovan introducing himself to Nick as Maggie shut the door. I lingered by the door, trying to listen in. I wondered how much Donovan was sharing with Nick.

"Come on, now, Annie, let's get you inside. Would you like some hot cocoa? Do you have any bags?"

She put her arm around me and ushered me inside. The guys stayed outside to talk for a bit. I assumed Donovan was bringing Nick up to speed on the situation. Since we hadn't talked since his revelations to me, I wasn't sure what was going on between us. I started to have a sinking suspicion that he only pretended to like me to find out more about my connection to Marcos and Harry.

After Maggie gave me brandy-laced hot cocoa and some scrambled eggs, she showed me to our room. Lizzy brought my bags up the stairs. She told me to make myself at home and promptly went back downstairs. The couch felt amazingly soft and I crashed hard.

When I woke up, the midday sun shone brightly into

the room. It took me a minute to remember where I was and why I was there. I looked around the room. Since the room was really Maggie and Nick's guest room, I saw that Lizzy hadn't put too much of her own personality into it. I knew that she didn't plan on living there for too long. To be honest, though, I did love how Maggie had decorated the room. The guest room had white woodwork with a roses theme. The walls were painted light brown and textured to look like suede. The mahogany highboy dresser held a vase filled with pink and yellow silk roses. The white bedspread had intricate rose-pink, cream, and brown stitching throughout. And the couch I slept on was under a beautiful Monet painting, of a couple standing near a little cottage in a bed of roses. The painting—well, print really—accented the wall perfectly. I could live in this room for a while.

Before I even got up, I heard a little squeak in the room. I looked over by the bed and saw an itty-bitty little girl staring at me. She must have been about three and had enormous blue eyes like her aunt Lizzy. She had twisty little blond pigtails and wore a pumpkin sweater. I would have thought she was a doll if I hadn't seen her blink.

"Hello," I said, smiling at her.

She waved at me, still clutching her stuffed bear. She looked oh-so-solemn.

"What's your name?"

"What yoursh?"

"I'm Annie. Is Maggie your Mommy?"

She nodded, very seriously. Her little pigtails bobbed with her head. She seemed to relax a little when I mentioned her Mommy. As if on cue, Maggie came rushing into the room.

"I saw your door opened, and guessed that you might have a little visitor," Maggie said breathlessly. "This is our little girl, Lucy. Lucy, say Hi to Annie. She's your aunt Lizzy's friend."

"Hi, Yannie."

I held out my hand for Lucy to grab. She grabbed one of my fingers and shook it.

"So good to meet you, Lucy." I smiled at her. She just nodded and kept staring at me. Then she smiled, and the sun came out. She had me hook, line, and sinker.

I threw my legs over the side of the bed. "Thank you for everything, Maggie. I didn't get much sleep last night. What time is it?"

"About one in the afternoon." She straightened up the room a little, and brought me a towel, washcloth, and clean toothbrush. "And it's no trouble at all! Donovan explained everything to Nick. And Lizzy explained you and Donovan to me," Maggie winked as she swept out of the room. Lucy followed her.

I got up, found my suitcase, and rummaged through it for something to wear. I found a red wool sweater and pair of jeans.

Maggie came back into the room with Lucy following close behind, and said, "The shower is just down the hall." She smiled and added, "Oh, and Lizzy asked me to tell you that she went to work, but she'll be back in time for dinner tonight."

With that, she grabbed Lucy's hand, and they left the room.

I grabbed the towel, washcloth, and clothes, and headed for the bathroom. I took a long shower to clear my head of these latest happenings. Letting the water cascade over me didn't give me any breakthrough, but I was feeling more like myself. Dressing quickly, I determined more than ever to figure out what I had stumbled—bumbled, more like—into.

Since I had time on my hands in the afternoon, I went over my notes for the case and tried to contact Marcos yet again. I wished I could go to the library to do some research but didn't have a car. Thoughts kept swirling around in my head, but I couldn't make any connections. The jewels hidden in the mug really stumped me. Idly, I wondered if Marcos' lawyer, Jim Donaldson, would know anything. Like most people, sometimes I think better when I let my mind wander while doing other things. So, I started playing with Lucy.

I was sitting in the kitchen, coloring with Lucy when Lizzy came home.

Lucy ran to Lizzy, shouting, "Yay, Auntie's here!"

"Hey, Lizzy! How are you?" I asked.

"Great. But I should ask how you are." She picked up Lucy and swung her around. "How's my little munchkin?" she asked Lucy, who answered with a giant giggle.

"Has everything been okay?" Lizzy lowered her voice, "M-A-G-G-I-E can be a bit B-O-S-S-Y." Lizzy spelled out some of the words for Lucy's benefit.

"Who can be B-O-S-S-Y, Lizzy?" Maggie asked as she joined us in the kitchen.

"Y-O-U can, but you know I love you," Lizzy went to hug her older sister.

Maggie gave a pretend grunt but hugged her back. From the little that Lizzy had shared, I gathered she and Maggie had a typical sisterly relationship. Ready to do battle with each other at a moment's notice, but woe be it to anyone who hurt the other. As an only child, I felt a pang of envy over their easy teasing.

"Hey, Maggie, what's for dinner? I'm famished. Oh, and Annie, you'll appreciate this. Guess who asked about you today?"

It couldn't be Donovan, he knew my whereabouts. "Who?"

"Mom's meatloaf."

Maggie and I spoke at the same time. I said, "Jinx, buy me a Coke," and we both laughed.

Slightly annoyed, Lizzy pointed out that we hadn't actually said the same thing, and you could only say "jinx" when you both said the same thing. Maggie rolled her eyes. Yep, typical sisters.

"I'm dying of curiosity, Lizzy! Who asked about me?"

Lizzy grabbed my arms and told me to brace myself, "You're not going to believe this!"

"Who? Who?"

"Mommy, did Annie turn into an owl?" Lucy innocently asked.

"No, sweetheart, your Aunt Lizzy is just teasing her. Would you just tell her already! I want to know too!"

"Okay. Okay. You guys are no fun! Cindy!"

"Cindy? Who's Cindy?" Maggie asked. Clearly, Lizzy hadn't brought that particular work problem home with her.

"Cindy asked about me? Why on earth would she? She barely acknowledged me while I lived at the Lighthouse."

"Who's Cindy?" Maggie tried again.

"I know, right? She barely acknowledged either of us, really. I was shocked she lowered herself to talk to me!"

"Who. Is. Cindy?" Maggie almost shouted. We both gaped at her, startled by the outburst. She wiped her hair off her brow. "Sorry, I got carried away. But who is this person? Does she figure into this whole thing?"

"I don't think so," I hedged. I couldn't help but add, "however, she certainly does act suspiciously."

"Oh, you don't really think she's involved, Annie, do you?"

"Well, who's to say? I mean, why is she so eager about knowing where I've gone?"

"Good point." Lizzy explained to Maggie Cindy's role at the inn and what had happened when Lizzy spilled the coffee on her.

"She sounds like a grump. But do you really think she could have committed murder?"

"Honestly, Maggie, I don't know what to think anymore."

Maggie pulled the meatloaf out of the oven. "Good thing you won't have to think for the next hour or so, then. Soup's on!"

The smell of garlicky mashed potatoes and tender

meatloaf made my mouth water, literally. A chopped salad rounded out the meal nicely. Nick led us in grace, otherwise he really didn't say much. For a few minutes, none of us said anything as we wolfed down the great dinner. Comfort food made for the ultimate balm.

"So, Annie, Lizzy told us you're from Milwaukee. How did you get involved with this project?" asked Maggie.

I told her about my ghostwriting projects and how I had started working for Harry while I attended Marquette University. Lizzy filled her in on exactly what had happened, up to my ransacked room. She did not mention the jewels. She, Kitty, and I had made a pact to not mention them to anyone else, except Donovan. At this point, we felt like we couldn't be too careful.

"So, someone went through your stuff? Poor Kitty, I bet she feels horrible about that."

"She does, but it wasn't her fault."

"I'm sure she was relieved to hear you say that."

"Oh, Annie, Kitty said she boxed up a few more of your things and you can pick them up whenever you want."

"Would it be okay if I went to work with you tomorrow?"

"To pick it up?"

"Yeah."

"Actually, if Nick gives me a ride to work, you can use my car and pick me up from work," Lizzy graciously offered. "Is that okay, Nick?"

"Sure, no problem," Nick said after swallowing a huge mouthful of mashed potatoes.

Everyone cleaned their plates, went back for seconds, and promptly fell into food comas. Except for Lucy. She ran around the living room, trying to get someone to play with her until Maggie and Nick corralled her for bath time and tucked her into bed. I couldn't help but think what a lucky little girl she was to have two parents who clearly loved her.

"She is so sweet," I said to Lizzy, as they went up the stairs.

"I know, she is a little sweetie-pie, isn't she? I love her to pieces."

"I can tell. It is really great of Maggie and Nick to open their home to me. Are they always this kind?"

"They are rare. I've even seen Maggie give a homeless woman the cardigan off her back." I stared at her in shock. A happy kind of shock.

"Really? Wow—I've never even heard of that before. Growing in Milwaukee was a lot different, I think," I said. "What about Nick?"

"Well, they met serving meals at the Salvation Army. They love to share the story that their hands met over a bowl of mashed potatoes and the rest is history." We oohed and awwwwed over the sweet story. Lizzy asked me about my family.

I shared the basic story. My Grandparents raised me after my Mom, Jo Ann Malone, died tragically at a very young age. Grandma died when I was about 13, and Aunt Helen moved in the following year. My story got a bit heavy and needed to be doled out in smaller chunks. It could overwhelm even the toughest person.

Lizzy and I stayed up until midnight chatting about our very different upbringings. It felt a lot like an old-fashioned slumber party.

•••

I woke up the next morning at my usual time of six thirty-ish. When I made it downstairs, Lizzy was already sitting with Nick and Lucy. Maggie was making pancakes with chocolate chips, which brought back fond memories of childhood. Except I used to sneak teaspoons of sugar with my pancakes.

Maggie had Lucy dressed like a ladybug.

"What's the occasion?" I asked, smiling at the little

ladybug.

"She wanted to wear her Halloween costume for you, so I let her," Maggie said. "She's taken quite a liking to you."

"Great pancakes, honey," said Nick. "Lizzy, I'll be ready to leave at seven, sound good?"

"Yep, I'm all set. Annie, can you pick me at four or so?"

"Sounds great."

When everyone else left for their jobs, and Lucy for daycare, I decided to clean the house for Maggie. She had been so kind to me, I felt it was a small way to give back to her and Nick. Lizzy had shown me where everything was yesterday evening, so I got to work.

I spent the rest of the day out of sight in the guest room, reading. Now if this was how I got to spend my time unemployed, I could get used to it. But once we found Harry's killer, I needed to buckle down and get a job. Idly, I wondered what kind of job I could find up in Door County, if I decided to stay after all this fiasco was put to bed.

•••

"Hey Annie! Welcome back!" came Kitty's exuberant greeting at the door when I arrived to pick up Lizzy. "I put your stuff in back. Oh, and I think George has a message for you." At that moment the phone rang. "Lighthouse Inn. Kitty speaking." Kitty waved me on as I headed towards the bar to get the message from George.

A message for me? Thoughts raced through my head. As I approached George at the bar, my heart soared at the hope I would hear the words, "Donovan called. He wants you to call him back right away." I was even prepared to be in a snit that he hadn't tried my cell phone. But, why would Donovan call for me at the Lighthouse Inn? He knows Lizzy's sister's number and my cell phone.

With my heart in my throat, I heard George's actual message for me, "Hey Annie! Good to see ya! I hope Lizzy's family is treating you okay. Joyce Limburger called for you."

I tried to ignore my heart falling to the pit of my stomach, as I scrunched up my face and asked, "Joyce?"

"Yeah, she said she's friends with Effie McInerny? I have her number here. She said it's real important." He put down the glass he was wiping and leaned across the bar, beckoning me closer. "Between you and me, kid, she sounded like a real pushy broad." He went on to tell me about their conversation.

I had a big soft spot for George. He reminded me of my Grandpa, but about 20 years younger. His eyes twinkled as he related how Joyce had demanded to speak to me. He seemed to take it in stride that she accused him of lying when he said I wasn't at the Lighthouse Inn anymore. In any case, he promised to get the message to me.

"Wow, I guess I'd better get back to her right away, huh?" I took the note he gave me with Joyce's number.

"Can't blame you if you don't," said George as he smiled. He turned to a bar customer, "What can I get you, sir?"

Turning away from the bar, I almost bumped into Cindy. She startled me—she came up behind me so quietly. On the practical side, I knew she probably had a bar order for George to fill. However, I couldn't help but think she had been listening in on our conversation. But why? Ever since Lizzy had accidentally spilled that coffee on her, she had been inexplicably rude to us.

So, when I almost smacked into her, I gasped. She muttered, "Watch out, Clumsy," as she put her tray on the bar. Shrugging off her increasingly (and unaccountably) odd behavior, I recovered quickly and said, "Hi Cindy! So sorry—I didn't see you there," before running back to the storage room. Lizzy had told me Kitty had put my stuff there.

As I made my way through the dining room and back hallway, I spotted Lizzy, who was very busy serving tables. Since it looked like all of her tables were full, I didn't linger. I'd have to wait for her tables to clear for a while before we could leave. Catching her eye briefly, I gave her a quick wave. On my way to the storage area, I heard footsteps behind me.

"Annie?" I recognized Millicent's gravelly voice and sighed, wondering what she wanted.

Turning to face her, I bit back a smart-aleck answer and said, "Yes, what can I do for you, Millicent?" Forcing a smile on my face, I willed myself to be nice to this woman and not let her bitterness affect me.

"I heard you wanted to talk to Joyce. I don't know what you expect to get from her, but she's a bit useless in the head." She tapped her own head to emphasize her point.

"She seemed fine to me." Why I wanted her to think I had talked to Joyce, I didn't know. Maybe to get Millicent's goat? All I knew was this, my gut was telling me that Millicent was warning me off talking to Joyce and I didn't know why.

"Well, that's the thing," Millicent hedged as she shifted uncomfortably to her other foot. "She seems okay, but I've known her since kindergarten and she's always been slow. She tries to make up for it by exaggerating." Hmmm, Millicent is not a great friend.

"Thanks for the tip, Millicent," I said, trying to slide away from her and towards the storeroom door. "I'll keep that in mind if I talk to her again." As politely as I could, I excused myself and practically sprinted the rest of the way to the storeroom.

Box in hand, I opted to slip out the back door. I headed back to Lizzy's car to call Joyce in private. I knew that Lizzy would want to come along for the interview.

Joyce answered on the first ring, "Hello?" came a soft-as-silk voice.

"Hello," I answered. "Is Joyce available?"

"This is she." Her? She sounded so sweet and calm. George was afraid of her? She sounded like a gently bred older lady.

"Hello, Joyce. This is Annie Malone," I began, only to have her cut me off.

"Oh, so Annie Malone is deigning to call me back," she sniped. Her gentle voice was greatly at odds with her crabby tones. I found the combination jarring. I silently thanked George for preparing me.

"I, um, well, I just got your message," and I thanked her for calling me so quickly, hoping to calm her. "And I was, uh, hoping that I could stop by to talk to you about the house across the street from you."

"Why do you want to talk about those troglodytes? They have been nothing but a headache for our neighborhood, digging holes, gallivanting all hours of the night."

I decided to give her the partial truth. "I'm ghostwriting book about a man named Marcos Landrostassis and I have reason to believe he might be one of those 'bums,' as you put it. I can't seem to reach him by phone. I figured if I could talk to his neighbors, I might be able to glean more info on him."

Just as I suspected it might, this appealed to Joyce's vanity. People liked to be "in the know." I could hear her preening over the phone. "You know, the things I could tell you about that house. What did you say his name is again, Marcos? Constantly, people are in and out of his house. Oh, of course, Marcos. He must be that dark-haired fella. Yes, that makes sense. Oh, he is very Greco-European looking, I think." Fortunately, Joyce couldn't hear me roll my eyes over the phone. She didn't miss a beat. "And he has women over all the time. He has at least five women after him."

"Wait. I thought he was married?"

"If he's married, he's even more of a scallywag than I thought. He seems to favor blondes."

"Is he that good looking?" I asked.

"Oh, heaven's no," Joyce laughed "He looks like a younger version of Abe Vigoda, but with hair." A small laugh escaped me. "You know who he is then, do you? No, I think the women were after," her voice dropped to a whisper, "his money and power."

"Power?" Keep in mind, I still wasn't sure we were talking about the same person. I hadn't met Marcos face-to-face and she didn't know if he definitely lived in that house. If anything, she seemed intent on confirming Millicent's allegations of exaggerating.

"Mob."

At that, she insisted she couldn't say more and invited me over.

Quickly I agreed, before she could change her mind. I wrote down her address (which was one house down from Effie's). Early afternoon would be perfect Lizzy could come along between shifts at the Lighthouse.

CHAPTER 18

"THANKS FOR GIVING ME A RIDE home," Lizzy said as she hopped into her car.

"Well, thank you for letting me borrow your Honda while they're fixing my brakes."

Lizzy pouted a bit, which was so unlike her, I blurted out, "What's wrong? Do you need your car back?"

"No, it isn't that. I'm not sure… it's just that…," she couldn't seem to get it out. Patiently, I waited. I had noticed that the sunsets were quite spectacular in Door County. While Lizzy organized her thoughts, I drove on and enjoyed the oranges, pinks, and purples streaking across the sky.

I whispered, "Amazing."

"Annie, I need to talk to you about something and I'm not sure how," Lizzy hesitated. "I mean, I know we've become fast friends, but we haven't known each other very long. Oh look! There's Janie's car!"

"Where?" I could see a winery-slash-wine bar just ahead on the right side of the highway.

"There!" Lizzy pointed to the wine bar's parking lot. "Let's go meet her. It'll be fun."

"Didn't you want to talk to me about something?"

"Wine can't hurt it," Lizzy replied as she smiled at me. Whew. Okay. I had been worried that I offended Lizzy somehow. Pulling into the parking lot, I parked as close to Janie's silver Volkswagen as I could.

As we headed into the wine bar, I insisted that Lizzy let me treat tonight.

"You are on! Thanks—what's the occasion?"

"Please! Isn't you letting me use your Honda enough of a reason?"

We made our way to the bar and ordered our wine. I got a wonderful Shiraz, and Lizzy got a yummy white zinfandel. Quickly spotting Janie and her companion, we found a table where we would see the whole room.

I poked Lizzy. "Did you know Janie was seeing anyone?"

"No idea. I wonder who he is, though. He's cute!"

I looked over at Janie and her date. They looked comfortably flirtatious together. His cool blond looks set off her exotic dark-haired beauty perfectly. Where Kitty looked a bit like a little sparrow, Janie's eyes slanted up a bit more, giving her a feline appearance

"Ahem. I said, 'Speaking of cute guys,'" Lizzy interrupted my thoughts.

"What? Oh, I'm sorry, I wasn't paying attention." I sighed a little, adding, "They look happy together."

"You could have that too."

"I could? With who? What are you talking about?"

"Oh look, they have tapas!" Lizzy exclaimed and tried to make a break for the appetizers. While I'll admit the appetizers looked delicious, I lightly grabbed her sleeve.

"Please, Lizzy, no more distractions. First, tell me what's up, please. I'm dying of curiosity."

"Okay, okay. Here it goes... what is going on between you and Donovan?"

I stared at her, open-mouthed. "There's nothing going on. We're friends, that's all."

"Okay, fine, be that way. But I see the way you light up

when you're around him."

Taking a sip of my drink, I avoided making eye contact with Lizzy. Part of me was annoyed with her for pointing out the attraction I felt but couldn't act on, and the other part of me was annoyed with myself for being so transparent. He was investigating this case and couldn't get personally involved.

Lizzy gently placed her hand on my arm, "Look, I really don't want to butt in, but why do you seem to be pushing Donovan away. The attention he pays to you even makes me blush."

At that moment, Janie and her escort came to our table.

"Hey, how are my two favorite sleuthers? Sleuthers? Is that a word? Anyway, Lizzy and Annie, I'd like you to meet Paul Wolff. Paul, this is Lizzy Holloway and Annie Malone."

We exchanged pleasantries as Janie and Paul found bar stools to sit with us awhile.

"So how long has Janie known you two?" He looked at Lizzy first.

Lizzy told him she'd become friends with Janie since working at the Lighthouse Inn, but had known of her before that because of their growing up in the area. When he looked at me, I explained that I was new to the area, but have loved getting to know Janie.

"I completely agree," he said, putting his arm around Janie's shoulders. "She is something special. And to think I almost didn't come up to Door County!" He gazed admiringly at Janie, who blushed prettily. With a flourish, he lifted his wine glass, and added, "To Janie!"

Janie blushed even more as we drank to her. For the next several minutes, we chatted and enjoyed our wine. I felt like we had walked onto a movie set, the whole scene seemed a little surreal. My life had changed so much in such a short time. Yet, other than the trauma of Harry's murder and the crazy client, I liked the changes.

Before going back to their own table, Janie looked over

at Paul and Lizzy. Paul was asking Lizzy some questions about the area. Janie whispered in my ear, "Don't worry about how things are with Donovan right now. I have a feeling that everything will work out just fine." Oddly, that quiet message gave me immediate peace about the situation.

Even so, I needed confirmation, so I whispered back, "How do you know?"

"Oh, sweetie, some things you just know. You know?" Smiling, she rose and said out loud, "We just wanted to stop by and say hi. Paul wanted to meet my dear friends. We'll leave you now."

We all hugged and said our good-byes. Paul steered Janie back to their table.

"What a great couple," Lizzy sighed. "I hope he's as good as he seems. Janie deserves some happiness. What did she tell you anyway?"

Now it was my turn to blush. "She told me to give Donovan another chance."

Lizzy looked at me sternly, and asked, "Are you going to now?" She teasingly added, "It's two against one."

"I'll see what I can do. You know, it isn't just up to me," I stated.

"Well, that's a given. Look, Annie, I've seen the way he looks at you. Why don't you call him right now?"

"Okay, I will," and quicker than quick, I grabbed my phone. I slid off my stool and made a dash for the entryway. I tried to call him but got his voicemail. I wasn't sure what kind of message to leave him. I mean, I wasn't completely sure of his feelings and didn't want to leave him a weird voicemail message. Resolving to borrow Lizzy's car after our winery stop, I figured I could stop by his house later that night.

Making my way back to our table, I had to clear a newly formed cluster of people. Someone jostled my arm and my phone flew through the air, landing a few feet away. A slightly smarmy guy grabbed my arm, saying with a slight accent, "Oh no! Are you okay? I'm so sorry. When I talk, I talk with my hands, you know?"

"Yes, I know." In spite of myself, I smiled, thinking of Lizzy's coffee encounter. "It's okay, I understand. But, have you seen my—?" Right then, one of Mr. Smarmy's friends, Mr. Too-White-Teeth presented me with a phone.

"Your phone?"

"Yes, whew! I don't know what I'd do without this!" Thanking them and shaking their hands, I finally got back to our seats. Lizzy had a plate piled with awesome tapas happiness. I decided to do the same.

Once I got some bruschetta, crudités, and chicken satay, I headed back to our table, and announced, "Now, back to matters at hand." I explained about our meeting with Joyce the next day, and asked Lizzy if I could borrow her car later that night to talk to Donovan.

She smiled at me, "No, you can't borrow my car." I must have looked shocked. "You can't borrow my car because Donovan is here."

•••

I turned around only to stand face to face with the subject of my thoughts perfectly clad in a dark blue shirt, jeans, and my absolute favorite black leather jacket. Well, now we had to talk.

"So, how do we do this?" I asked Donovan.

"I say I'm sorry and tell you I can't get you out of my head," said Donovan.

"I suppose that sounds reasonable. When you didn't stop in and say 'Hi' at Maggie and Nick's, I wasn't sure if you really liked me or were just using me for information."

"I know, but you understand my position, right?"

My ability to speak left me as I stared up into his gorgeous eyes. Shyly, I put my head down and nodded lightly.

Donovan held up his hands in mock surrender. "Annie,

one thing does bother me about you, actually."

"Me?"

"Yes, you. Are you the real thing? I find it hard to believe that a woman as pretty as you gets flustered so easily."

I just gaped at Donovan in disbelief.

"Oh c'mon, don't tell me no one has ever told you how lovely you are? You cannot expect me to believe that!"

"Actually, only my Aunt Helen has ever told me. And I thought she was just being prejudiced."

"Really?"

"Yep. Ahem. Well, anyway, before I lose my nerve, I have a question for you." I needed to get the question out quickly before my blush burned my ears off. I had never had a conversation like this. Growing up in an overprotective family had led to me being a little more sheltered than the average twenty-two-year-old woman. Since moving out on my own, I had shed some of that naiveté, but my natural tendencies leaned toward protecting myself by staying in a sort of a cocoon. Donovan jolted me out of my comfort zone, which was part of what attracted me to him.

"Ahem... are you still going to ask your question?" Donovan broke into my thoughts. "I await your question with bated breath."

"Oh, I'm sorry. I have a lot on my mind, which is part of my question."

"I'm intrigued and getting more intrigued by the minute."

I took a big gulp of air and just rushed out with, "Oh, this is just so silly!"

"I'm sure it isn't silly. C'mon, what do you want to know?"

"Who called you when you left the bar that night?"

"Ooooh, that night?"

Too late, I was bright red. Clearing my throat, I croaked out, "Yes, the night you wanted to see my manuscript."

"Weren't there notes? There were supposed to be notes, too," Donovan whispered, staring deeply into my eyes.

"Donovan!" I stomped my foot in mock protest.

"Okay, okay. What do you want to know about that night?"

"Who called you at the bar? Why did you leave?"

"The mechanic. I had told him to call me if he uncovered anything suspicious about your little, ahem, accident. Anyway, that call was the police station telling me that a detective had just gotten back from the mechanic. As a professional courtesy, the detective confirmed what we already knew—that the brake line was cut."

So, he didn't leave me to talk to some other woman! My insides did cartwheels. I tried to keep my face calm, as I smiled up at him. Oddly, the real reason for that call was the best news I had gotten in a long while.

"Well, I'm glad to hear that."

"I'm glad you're glad. What do you say to a proper date once we catch Harry's killer? In the meantime, I know I shouldn't do this, but I have a favor to ask you. Would you mind coming with me to interview Tina Delvecchio?"

"What? Really?" I knew my eyes had lit up like a Christmas tree. "Do you need her address or something? Because I don't have it. I thought you PI guys had connections."

Wryly, he said, "I have her address, Annie. She lives in Michigan City now. I'd like to have you along because you are familiar with her story and involvement with Marcos."

Humbled, I responded, "Oh."

"Well, will you?"

Feeling I might have shown too much excitement, I tried to downplay it a little, "Sure that sounds good. What time should I be ready?"

"I'll come to get you at ten, okay?"

"I look forward to that and our real date very much."

"Good night, Annie." He kissed my forehead. "I'm sorry this last week has been kind of tough on you."

"Thanks. Do you think we'll ever find Marcos?"

"That is the sixty-four-thousand-dollar question, isn't it?"

I smiled at him, and looked down, "Good night, Donovan."

"Don't stay up too late with your buddies."

I turned and walked back to the wine shop. Halfway there, I turned back around to wink and smile at Donovan.

"You're killin' me, Annie Malone!" I heard him cry as I continued to walk away. I tried to put a little sway in my hips. *What am I doing?* I thought as I reached the door. It didn't even hit me until much later that night, I never even asked him why he showed up at the wine shop.

CHAPTER 19

PROMPTLY AT TEN, THE WILLIAMS' doorbell rang. I had made sure to be ready before Donovan could uninvite me. I knew he was worried about increasing my involvement, but I also knew that he needed my help with what Marcos had told me about Tina Delvecchio.

He kept his face very stern as he greeted me, which only made him look hotter. I smiled.

"Um, Donovan, I have an idea."

He looked at my lips, and said, "So do I." *Oh my.*

"I thought you didn't want to do anything like that right now?" I teased.

"You're right, you're right. There will be time enough for that later." *My oh my.* Discreetly, I fanned my face a bit.

I locked the door after us, and we promptly left.

Rain and leaves came down in sheets. The wind blew around us as we ran for the car.

Once we got to his car, he asked me what my idea was. I told him about the harassment Marcos had gotten from the cops, and Tina Delvecchio's part in the drama.

"Oh, yeah, I remember reading something about that in the file. Do you think she's worth talking to?" A thrill shot through me that he valued my opinion.

"Well, it isn't so much what he told me that happened, per se. But when I suggested interviewing her for the book, he went nuts!"

His eyes narrowed, "Did you just remember this now?"

"Hey, it has been a rough couple of days. Anyway, when I brought up interviewing her, to get the full story on Marcos and his family, he almost came through the phone."

A shiver went through me. The enormity of the danger I was in struck me. Until we found Marcos, I would not be safe.

"Where does she live anyway?"

"Near the docks in Michigan City."

As we headed down Highway 42, I started to relax again. I felt like everything might be all right, after all.

She seemed to live in a rundown neighborhood. The grey day only made the neighborhood look more dismal. An empty lot near her house was covered in weeds and littered with beer bottles. I thought I even saw a syringe on the ground. The brown trim of her duplex needed a fresh coat of paint, and the mustard yellow siding could have used a good power-washing. I sniffed the air. It smelled like someone had something burning nearby. But not that good kind of autumnal, fireplace burning. It smelled more like that bad kind of falling asleep smoking on a mattress kind of burning. I didn't see a burned out, soggy mattress in any of the front yards, but I would lay money on there being a recently-doused mattress fire in one of the backyards.

"When we get to her house, let me do the talking, okay?" Donovan said.

"Why? I know the story that Marcos told me, you don't. You only know what I told you." I didn't mean to challenge him, but I had a valid point.

He ran his fingers through his hair. "Are you always this difficult?"

"Only when I think I'm right." I gave him what I hoped was a winning smile.

"All right. I'll do most of the talking, but you can jump in," he said as he pressed the doorbell. No answer. No footsteps. No signs of life.

He pressed the doorbell again. Still no response. The roof overhang offered little protection from the rain. We were both rapidly becoming soaked.

Then he knocked on the door.

We heard faint footsteps. "I'm comin', I'm comin'. Hold on to your shorts," sounded a raspy voice on the other side of the door.

The door flew open, almost hitting me in the nose. I stepped back reflexively.

"Yeah, what do ya want?" Tina Delvecchio had not worn well with age. Years of alcohol abuse, cigarettes, and possible drug usage had not treated her well. She looked about 65, but I guessed her age was more like 45, based on the timeline Marcos had given me. The few teeth she had left were hanging on for their little, yellow lives. Her limp grey hair hung around her face, which looked sallow and puffy. Her bloodshot eyes were more red than brown. She wore a pink-striped housecoat, with mysterious stains in various places. And, her fuzzy slippers looked like they may have started out as white, but had become suspiciously yellow over time. She looked like a Halloween costume, but I didn't think her look could be duplicated. The cigarette dangling from her mouth as she talked only added to her dubious charms.

Donovan cleared his throat. "Are you Tina Delvecchio? We need to talk to you about Marcos Landrostassis."

"That's me. What's it to you, anyways?"

"He's missing, and we have reason to believe he is connected to certain activities."

"Oh, really? Humpf, that guy really gets around," she cackled. "I thought he was curtailing his activities. He really got into a lot of trouble when he tried to steal that dog."

"Actually, he's involved in something a lot worse than dognapping."

"My, oh my. That Marcos sure could get himself in a pickle." She cackled again. She was clearly on something.

"I was wondering about his actions during your time as his tenant," I chimed in. "What happened to Ray Harris?"

"You want to begin at the beginning, do you? All right, you might as well come on in."

Donovan whispered, "Good job."

She lived in the bottom half of the duplex. Her apartment looked like it came straight off the show about hoarders. Well, maybe that's a little harsh. Her place could have been on a show called Hoarders Lite. Miscellaneous garbage littered the floor. Tina's dog was eating out of the cat's litter box. I had to cover my nose discreetly with my hand against all the bad smells. I caught a whiff of rotting meat and almost lost it.

"Steady, Annie," Donovan said, out of the corner of his mouth. "So, Ms. Delvecchio, when did you last see Marcos?"

"Lemme think… the bank took over that place about two years ago and kicked us all out."

"Us all? Who do you mean?"

"Myself and the Landrostassis family."

"Oh right. Do you know where Marcos and Diana went to live after that happened?"

"She went to live with her parents somewhere in Illinois. He went to jail for the dognapping."

"Perhaps we should explain ourselves a little better. Miss Malone here," Donovan gestured to me. "She was hired to ghostwrite a story for Marcos to prove his innocence because he was convinced the cops were in collusion with the bank against him."

"Well, I'll tell you one thing. Whatever that fool told you is wrong. I would have done anything for him."

What was she talking about? Did she mean Marcos? As she spoke, I noticed a picture on her wall of a vibrant, gorgeous blonde on the arm of a dark-haired man. Discreetly, I poked Donovan and pointed to the picture. His mouth almost dropped open, but he kept his cool. I assumed that was Tina when times were better.

"Ms. Delvecchio, what happened the night Ray Harris was stabbed?" I needed to find out more about Marcos. The minute I had started working on this project, I had felt uneasy. Now, Marcos was missing, and my editor was dead. I sensed that Tina knew more than she let on.

"Ray Harris? I don't know anybody by that name. What are you talking about?" She gave me the stink eye. I cringed a little. Then I saw a cockroach crawling across an empty pizza box on her coffee table, and I almost threw up.

Donovan gave me a warning look.

He took over the questioning again. "When you lived as Mr. Landrostassis' tenant, do you remember any late night visits from anyone associated with Dmitri Tasios?"

I couldn't hide my shock. Dmitri Tasios? Everyone knew that name. Dmitri Tasios headed up a Greek version of the mob. He was elusive, though, and stayed just out of the clutches of the law. So, was Marcos associated with Dmitri Tasios? What the actual f—?

"Nope, and even if I did, do you think I'd tell you?" She cackled again, then fell into a stupor. We waited several minutes while she sat there with her mouth open. Her eyes didn't even blink. Finally, we got up, convinced our interview was over, when she snapped out of it, stood up, and started shouting at us in Italian.

As she led us to the door, she whispered in my ear, "Come back tomorrow afternoon without the copper."

I tried to explain he wasn't a cop, but thought it might be safer for me if she was mistaken.

She started shouting in Italian again. We got out of there, fast.

The rain had died down a little, but the leaves were still falling en masse. Donovan and I got in his car and peeled out of there.

"What did she say to you as we were leaving?"

"She thought you were a cop. She said she wanted to talk to me without you there tomorrow afternoon."

"Dammit. I thought she was playing up the crazy bit a little too much."

"So, should I go?"

"Hell yes. Are you scared to go without me?"

"No, not really. She's really odd, but I think she's got something important to tell me. Marcos got so upset when I just mentioned interviewing her. Do you think she knows where he is?"

"I would guess not. But what would you think if I told you that was Marcos in that picture?"

"I would think, 'what the what'! Are you sure?"

"Positive. In the only picture I've seen of Marcos, he looked a little older, but the basic features are the same."

"But he claimed this undying love for his Diana! What gives?"

"Yeah, this case is like an onion, that's for sure."

"Do you know what she was saying in Italian?"

"Nope, but if I had to guess, I would say gibberish."

"I thought I was going to toss my cookies in her apartment."

"Yeah, I know. You turned a bit green."

As we made our way up the highway, I remembered that I needed to meet Lizzy at the Lighthouse Inn. I chewed on my lip wondering how I could broach the subject with Donovan. He was going right past the Lighthouse; he could easily drop me off. But if he knew we were going to interview someone without him, he wouldn't like it. We were going either way, but I didn't want to face a lot of awkward questions from him.

I decided to sidestep the truth a bit, "Kitty called me this morning and said that I had left a couple of things behind when I picked up my stuff yesterday. Would you mind if we stop at the Lighthouse?"

"Sure. Say, since it's about eleven-thirty, do you want to grab some lunch?"

"I would really enjoy that."

When we got to the Lighthouse Inn, we were immediately seated. It turned out that Cindy was our server. With borderline civility, Cindy took our drink orders and slapped down our menus. Donovan ordered iced tea and I got a diet soda.

"What's up with her?" Donovan asked, jerking his thumb towards the kitchen door that Cindy went through.

"All I know is Lizzy accidentally spilled coffee on her and she's never gotten over it." I shrugged. I shut the menu. "I know what I want."

"What are you having?"

"A big, juicy hamburger. With fries."

"Awesome. You like to eat."

"Of course I like to eat. I like meat, but I do like salads too. I just know that the hamburgers here are fantastic."

"You sold me. I'll have a burger and fries, too." And with that, Donovan shut his menu.

Cindy reappeared seconds later with our drinks. She gave us each a hostile sneer.

"What do you want?" she grumbled.

I stared in shock at my drink, unsure of what to do. I saw something in my soda that I did not expect to see. I didn't even hear Donovan order his lunch.

"Annie? Annie, it's your turn."

"My turn? I need to order, don't I?" Cindy took my order, but she certainly didn't smile about it.

Lowering my voice to a whisper, I grabbed Donovan's arm, and said, "There is a red hair in my soda!"

"A red hair? We should probably let Cindy know. She can get you a new soda."

"No, no, don't say anything. She'd probably spit in it or something. But where could the hair have come from?"

"Maybe it was in the air? From another customer?"

"Remember that dream I had? Maybe this is part of that."

Donovan was saved from making a reply by Lizzy appearing suddenly.

"I thought I heard you were both here! Did you find out anything?" Lizzy asked.

"Nope. Nothing to report," said Donovan. "Hey, Lizzy, when do you get off work?"

"Oddly, Kitty only scheduled me to twelve-thirty today. I'll be done about the time you finish lunch."

Donovan looked a bit sheepish and asked Lizzy if she could give me a ride back to her sister's. Apparently, he had forgotten an appointment in Anchor Harbor when he agreed to stay for lunch.

I couldn't resist teasing him a little, "So, you forgot all about work because you were distracted by me?" Exaggeratedly, I batted my eyes at him.

Very seriously, Donovan looked into my eyes and said, "Yes, that is exactly what happened."

Lizzy fanned herself and left us. And, once again, I blushed to my hair roots.

CHAPTER 20

FTER LIZZY FINISHED UP AT THE LIGHTHOUSE, we left for our appointment with Joyce Limburger.

"You have Joyce's address, right?" Lizzy asked, as we got into the car.

I pulled a piece of paper out of my pocket and waved it. "Got it right here! Although, we don't really need it, since she's next door to Effie. You know, I'm really hoping this is the breakthrough we need. I've tried to look for Jim Donaldson's information and have hit a brick wall there, too. I wish I knew what happened to Marcos!"

Ever the optimist, Lizzy practically bounced in her seat. "This is so exciting!" She started her Honda. "We are off then!"

On the way to Joyce's, I filled Lizzy in on my initial impressions of Joyce. Casually, I mentioned her frenemy standing with Millicent. Lizzy laughed when I told her about Millicent's take on her so-called friend's observations. Still laughing, Lizzy added, "Yeah, that sounds like sour old Millicent."

We got to Joyce's with ten minutes to spare. The house kind of resembled a gothic castle on the outside.

"So, what strategy should we use?" Lizzy asked as she parked the car. "Good cop, bad cop?"

For some reason Lizzy's question reminded me of what I had told Joyce. I snapped my fingers and exclaimed, "Oh, darn it all! I forgot a camera!" I explained what I had told Joyce about the reason for our visit.

Lizzy applauded my quick thinking, and added, "Well, today is your lucky day, Miss Annie Malone."

Getting out of the truck, she went around to the back and popped open the door. Lifting up a floor cover, she pulled out a professional looking camera. "Did you know I was into photography?"

Mouth agape, I shook my head. Stunned by the amazing coincidence, I said, "Maybe you mentioned it in passing, but I can't recall. This is great!"

We trudged up the sidewalk. I saw Effie's curtain twitch a little and felt oddly comforted to know she was watching us approach Joyce. I realized she wasn't watching out of any sense of protecting us, but blatant nosiness. However, it felt good just the same. The closer we got to the door, the more my stomach started to twist.

As I rang the doorbell, I asked Lizzy, "So, what do you think she looks like?"

"Hard to guess. Since she's clearly vain, probably not like Millicent."

"I know. Poor Millicent. There must be a good reason for her bitterness."

"There is," Lizzy said knowingly. "I'll tell you sometime. Are you sure she was expecting us at one?"

"Positive." I tried the bell again. "She suggested the time, actually." I knocked on the door this time, and it popped open. I looked at Lizzy in amazement, adding, "I did not knock on it that hard!"

Remember that stomachache I had mentioned? Add to that a chill going up my spine. I couldn't ignore that. Turning to Lizzy, I asked, "Do you think we should go in?"

"Yes," Lizzy said, and I thought I caught a hint of false bravado. But that could've been my own nerves I was sensing.

"Why do I sense something's wrong?"

"Yeah, I do too."

"What do you think we'll find?"

"I don't know. But we need to bite the bullet."

"Oh, why oh why did you say bullet?"

I gulped. Taking the bull by the horns, I called out, "Joyce?" through the open door. Getting the strongest sense of *deja vu*, I almost ran back to the truck. I could not shake the scene at the Lighthouse Inn, when I found Harry. I looked over at Lizzy, who stood right behind me in the doorway. She waved me forward, as if to say, "Get on with it."

Clearly a curious person, Lizzy did not seem quite as nervous as I felt. Of course, Lizzy hadn't found a dead body in the last week or so.

"Okay, okay, I'm going," I said, moving forward with the speed of a turtle on barbiturates. Lizzy gave me a little push. I stumbled forward into the entryway.

Once we got through the doorway, Lizzy pushed past me and fully into Joyce's foyer. "Wow, would you just look at this place? Heads R' Us, or what?"

Staring down from two-story high walls, I counted three bear heads, five bucks, and ten fish. Mounted game really freaked me out—those glassy eyes staring at me. Shiver. I deduced Joyce must be a kind of antique weapons expert, too. Either that or a dominatrix. Hatchets, bows and arrows, and spears also hung on the walls. Wait! Was that a blunderbuss? I had to give her credit—I was not expecting this decor, but I supposed it matched the castle-gothic feeling of the exterior. On the far side of the room stood a staircase that must have gone up to the bedrooms.

"Let's go upstairs and see if we can find her," Lizzy whispered. Her voice echoed through the entryway.

"Do you really think we should?"

Lizzy thought about it for a minute. I watched her eyes move as she went through several scenarios. "Yes, I think we should. What if she was taking a bath and she fell and broke her hip or something? I really would hate to think that we could have helped her but didn't because we were scared."

"Wait? Are you scared, too? I thought you weren't at all. You have really held it together well."

"Thanks, it has been an effort. Did the sky just darken, like, a lot? Are those animals freaking you out, too?"

"I'm not sure which is worse, those or the hatchets. Come on, you brought up a good point. Let's head upstairs."

At that moment, a clap of thunder roared overhead. Through Joyce's skylight, we saw a bolt of lightning split the sky. Talk about atmosphere! It looked like the lightning struck right over us.

We stood paralyzed at the base of the staircase. Gathering up every bit of courage I had, I said, "Okay, let's go now."

"Yeah, we really should go now." Yet neither of us could move. Another strike of lightning hit overhead.

On the floor behind us, we heard something scamper across the room. By the time we heard the second something scamper, we were halfway up the stairs. Caught between a rock and a hard place, we continued our upward motion to the "hard place."

Directly opposite the staircase was a closed door. I reached over, about to open it. Lizzy grabbed my hand and shook her head. I don't know if she had some sixth sense or something, but she whispered, "Don't touch anything."

"Right. Good point," I whispered back. "So, which way do we go?" Doorways lined the wall from either side of the staircase.

"Let's go… right."

"Right, it is."

We continued to tiptoe down the hallway. The storm

grew outside. Boom! A clap of thunder. Wow, that sounded close. The whole day had begun to take on a very eerie atmosphere, and the day was nowhere near over.

"Okay, seriously, if she were hurt," Lizzy asked, "wouldn't we have heard her by now?"

I shrugged. "Maybe she's unconscious. Is that a light coming out of the doorway?" I pointed to the last doorway on the side of the hall.

"Yep." Lizzy quickened her step and got there before me. By the time I got there, her face was ashen and she was focused on racing past me down the hallway. She looked like she was about to lose her breakfast. *Uh oh.* I peeked in the door.

On a big oak, four-poster bed, a very blue Joyce Limburger was laid out, almost in a funeral pose. From all of the mystery novels I had read, I assumed cyanide poisoning. She was wearing her pajamas and almost looked peaceful. Ugh. Super creepy. I ran into the room and felt her neck in vain to check her pulse. Nothing. I looked back towards the doorway for Lizzy. Also nothing. Then I heard the front door slam. I hoped she had made it outside in time. Figuring I should go check on Lizzy (you know, since she was probably in shock and there was nothing I could do for Joyce anyway), I pulled my phone out of my pocket as I ran down the stairs and out the door.

The rain came down in sheets. Although the storm had lessened, it didn't seem like the rain would let up anytime soon. Immediately, I spotted Lizzy in the front yard, doubled over. Relieved that I hadn't fainted this time, I dialed 911 on my cell phone and hit Send, expecting to be connected to an emergency operator.

KABOOM!!!!!

Darkness.

CHAPTER 21

WAS SOMEONE WATERBOARDING ME? Why was water pelting me, but I wasn't moving? Could I move? I moved my arms. They seemed okay. I moved my legs. They seemed okay. Tentatively, I opened my eyes, which stung a little. I could see okay, and I realized rain was falling on me. I saw the emergency vehicles in the distance, coming towards us.

Frantically, I sat up and looked around for Lizzy. I saw her lying in an odd position a few feet away from me and raced over to her. From what I had always learned about accidents, the number one rule is to not move an injured person unless necessary. So, I didn't move her, but I did satisfy myself that she had a pulse. The real shock was when I turned back around towards the house. Er, what was left of the house. What was left of the house was a smoldering heap with small fires here and there. Fires? What on earth had happened? The last thing I remembered was finding Joyce, racing out of the house, and calling 911. Er, trying to call 911. Wait? I don't remember speaking to an operator. So, if I didn't call 911, who did?

And, seriously, what happened to the house? Oh my

gosh, most of the house was gone, with bits and pieces of it strewn all over the yard. How did that happen? And when did it happen? I tried to piece the events together, but I had no idea how long I'd been laying on the lawn. I walked over to a smoking pile of something and had to cover my mouth from the harsh smell.

By the time the fire trucks pulled up, the rain had almost put out the fires. The air was filled with acrid smoke as thick as a fog. Why were my ears ringing? By now, the ambulances had arrived. The EMTs went immediately to Lizzy. Running over to them, I tried to communicate but couldn't understand what they were saying. Every sound felt gauzy. Her eyes were closed as they worked on her.

"Is she okay?" I asked them.

Unfortunately, my ability to read lips is almost nonexistent, so I didn't know what the EMT's answer was. I do know this; at my inability to hear him, I became panicked. I started yelling for my friend. One of the female EMTs guided me to an ambulance where they gave me oxygen and checked my ears.

Putting two and two together, I realized something must have happened to cause temporary (I hoped) hearing loss. After sitting on a stretcher near the ambulance for about 20 or so minutes, the rain began to taper off. Looking out at the lawn, I saw Effie moving towards me. I beckoned her over, patting a seat next to me.

I think I might have yelled this, but I said, "Hi Effie, do you know what happened?"

"Yes, don't you?" is what I think she said. My hearing was starting to return. I shook my head.

"Please tell me. I remember leaving the house, but nothing after that."

"Well, let's see. I saw you and that tall girl... What's her name again?" I could barely make out what she was saying.

"Lizzy. Can you please talk a little louder?"

She practically yelled, but I could definitely hear her,

"Oh, that's right. I keep remembering her caked in dirt and mud. I almost didn't recognize her. I didn't realize she was a blonde. But then I saw you and I recognized you immediately." She stopped to hack up a hairball. "Sorry about that."

"Ah, maybe you should get that checked out," I tried to suggest as delicately as I could. I thought she was about to cough up a lung.

"Tut. Tut. I'm fine. Ninety years old and fit as a fiddle." She looked at the imploded house, "Oh good. It looks like the fire is under control. Anyway, I saw you two girls arrive and go into the house. I figured Joyce let you in. By the way, I'm glad I could put you in touch with her."

"Thanks again," I muttered, noticing for the first time that my jeans were slightly singed.

"Oh, not a problem. Glad to do it. Anyway, I went back to the kitchen to start my tea. When I came back to the living room, I saw that tall, skinny one—Lizzy, right? Anyway, I saw her racing out of the house like a madwoman. Then I saw her lose her breakfast, in a manner of speaking. So, I put on my shoes and was about to come outside when I saw you dialing your phone, then BOOM!"

"What blew up?"

"See for yourself." She gestured towards the second story of the castle-lette. Or, what had been the second story. "It looked pretty amazing. The fire never really made much headway, what with the rain and all. You dialed, then the house's top blew off. I have never seen anything like it!" She chuckled a little, then sobered up. "Did Joyce make it out of the house in time?"

"Um, I hate to break this news to you, Effie, but Joyce was dead before the house blew up."

"What? I know she wasn't a pleasant woman, but who would kill her? Did you find her?"

"Not me," I said, pointing to Lizzy. "She did."

By this time, Lizzy was able to sit up.

"Tsk, tsk, that's a shame. When the boom happened, Lizzy got knocked into next week and her heavy camera fell on her arm. I think since you're smaller (and don't have as far to fall), you didn't get as hurt. Does your head hurt?"

"It did, but it feels better," I said, touching it gingerly. "Say, uh, Effie, when the dust settles a little on this, can I stop by to talk to you more about this latest event?"

"Sure, no problem, Annie. Tsk, tsk, tsk. Well, I am sorry about Joyce. She was a real pill, but she always knew everything about everybody. Let me go get you some lemonade." And before I could say it wasn't necessary, she was gone.

Watching Effie walk back to her house, I didn't notice Detective Chad Dupah approach me.

"Miss Malone?"

Recognizing his voice, I winced.

"Miss Malone, may I have a word?"

Reluctantly, I turned around, smiling sweetly. "Yes, detective?"

"What exactly happened here? Give me the Cliffs Notes version."

I gave the summarized version of our unfortunate visit to Joyce Limburger. He listened intently, his beady eyes searching mine for any lie. I told him what Effie told me, too. I explained how she told me that she saw me dial my phone and how the second floor exploded.

"Why were you talking to a neighbor of Marcos Landrostassis? What business do you have with Joyce Limburger?"

A little shiver when up my back when the detective indicated that it was Marcos' house across the street. I tried not to smile. I didn't want to give myself away. I drew myself up to my full (and unimpressive) height and said, "What do you care?"

"Given the fact that you and Lizzy 'found' (and, yes, he did do air quotes) Joyce, then the second floor of the house exploded, I think I have a right by law."

I put up my hands in mock surrender. "Honestly, I didn't even know it was Marcos' house until you just told me." Of course, there was no way I would tell him the real reason of our visit. I could tell him a variation of the one we told Joyce.

"As you know, I am working on that ghostwriting project for Marcos. Anyway, I haven't been able to get in touch with him since Harry's death. This book is my job, so I need to find out what's going on with it. I had this address in the notes Harry gave me. I was hoping that if I came to the house, I would be able to find out more information about the book's status, somehow." (A little embellishment, but it wasn't a lie.)

Chad grunted. "Do you know what happened to your phone?"

"No, it must have blown out of my hand during the explosion or implosion? Well, during the whatev—"

Detective Dupah cut me off.

"It did, Annie," he said. Looking at me very seriously, he asked, "Are you sure that was your phone? Have you dropped your phone recently, or had it with you in a crowded room?"

"Hey, Annie? These guys are taking me to the hospital. Can you let my sister know? Here's my keys," Lizzy said from her stretcher. The paramedics carried her close enough for me to get the keys.

"Wait, I'll follow you. Detective, are we through here?"

Sighing, Dupah said, "For now, but…"

We said in unison, "don't leave town."

Again, I smiled sickening sweetly at Detective Dupah, then turned around to catch up with Lizzy's stretcher. I heard him yell something after me, but all I could make out was the word phone. By the time they got her safely strapped in and we left, the fire had been completely put out. As I pulled away from the curb, I looked in the rearview mirror and saw a blonde head peeking out of

Marcos' front room window. Was that Diana? And what had she seen? How would I be able to interview her?

Frantically, I checked for my phone, then realized that's what Chad Dupah was trying to tell me.

By the time we got to the hospital, it was after noon. Lizzy's sister worked as a kindergarten teacher at the grade school in Turtle Bay, so I called the school to page her. Once she got to the phone, I explained what had happened. She said she just needed to make arrangements for Nick to pick up Lucy and tell her principal she needed to leave, and that she'd be there soon. I reiterated that fortunately it wasn't an emergency—Lizzy was conscious and could move. To be honest, they were more worried she had broken her wrist.

After I finished with Maggie, I asked one of the nurses for an update on Lizzy. She couldn't give me specific information (you know, patient privacy and all), but she did tell me that Lizzy was undergoing some tests and should be in her room soon. I grabbed a vending machine coffee and a magazine announcing the Monica Lewinsky scandal in the Clinton White House. Well, glad to see they kept up with the times. I settled into the waiting room and prepared to wait.

While flipping through the magazine from 1998, I heard my name called. When I looked up, I saw Donovan and my stomach did a little flip. Then I saw two guys in all black flanking him.

"Hey Annie, I need to talk to you about what happened."

"Sure," I said, putting down my magazine, "What do you need to know?" Since he had appeared with some colleagues, I figured I'd take his lead.

"Well, for starters, why were you talking to Marcos' neighbor?" His eyes bore into mine, daring me to tell him the truth.

As much as I hated to do it, I would have to tell him the same version of the truth I'd been telling.

"And don't tell me you were checking up on Marcos Landrostassis for the book. I know what you and Lizzy have been doing."

I turned white. Had he read my mind? I doubled down on my story. "But, honestly, I do need to find Marcos. As you know, this project is my bread and butter! I need to (I really emphasized 'need') find out what's going on with this book."

"Humpf," was all he said. I waited in vain for him to say something else for a full five minutes. Finally, he cleared his throat and began. "Since you have put yourself in the way of danger yet again, myself or one of these gentlemen will now be watching over you. You have obviously uncovered something important and my client needs you kept safe."

"Really? But I don't know who killed Harry!"

He held up his hand. "Stop. Whether you and Lizzy realize it or not, you do know something. I'll need you to share everything you've discovered so far. And you and Lizzy will need to be guarded from now until the cops find Harry's killer and whoever swapped out your phone."

"Swapped out my phone? Oh, of course, Dupah must have suspected it—that's why he asked if my phone had gone missing!"

"Yes, and if you and Lizzy had stayed in the house, we would not even be having this conversation. We wouldn't be having any conversation." He looked at me rather sternly, adding, "You both could have been blown sky high."

My heart fluttered a bit at this small measure of proof he cared about me.

"What was that?" I asked again. He knew exactly what I meant.

"It was a remote phone bomb. They swapped out your phone somehow with a detonated one. They had it wired to go off when you tried to contact the police."

"How much danger am I in?"

"Quite a bit, actually."

"The weird thing is, I had dreamt of a phone bomb a few nights ago," I admitted.

"Really?" Donovan asked, skeptically. "Not that I believe in that stuff, but what else did you dream?"

Immediately, my face turned bright red as I recalled the dream-kiss we shared. Instead, I said, "I dreamt that Harry came back and told me to 'Beware of the redhead'."

"Do you know any redheads?"

"No. Nor do I have any reason to be wary of them."

"Well, there you have it."

"Have what?"

"Well, you just proved my point about being skeptical over dreams. That's all."

I grunted in reply. There was still something I wanted to know from Donovan.

"How could Lizzy and I have bumbled into something like this? We were just doing some amateur sleuthing," I said. Clamping my hand over my mouth, I looked away in mortification. Crap, I had just told him what we were doing.

I heard footsteps retreating and assumed Donovan had grown tired of my silliness and left. Suddenly, I felt a hand tilt my face up.

"Look, Annie, in the short time I've known you, you've managed to work your way into my heart. I've grown to appreciate your quirky and fun self. I'm not sure where we're headed, but I'd like you to stay in one piece. Leave this case to the professionals. Considering what happened today, I've changed my mind about you meeting with Tina Delvecchio too. Clearly, our meeting with her today has alerted someone to our investigations. We must be getting too close for comfort."

Although his words thrilled me emotionally, I still wanted to get to the bottom of Harry's murder. Oh, and figure out why I had been given a mug with jewels embedded in it.

"Hey, now, don't be bummed. I promise, I w-," Donovan began. At that moment, Maggie found us.

"Annie, Annie! Where is she? Can I see her?" she asked, not even noticing Donovan at first. She grabbed me and hugged me like a rag doll. She actually picked me up.

Donovan, realizing the situation, winked at me, and opted to exit Stage Left. Darn it, what was he about to say?

"It's okay. Lizzy's gonna be fine," I reassured Maggie, returning the hug. "Um, can you put me down?" In her anxiety, Maggie had picked me up completely, to the amusement of some of the nurses.

"I'm sorry, I'm just so nervous, ya know? Other than Nick and Lucy, Lizzy's my only family up here since we lost our folks. Oops, sorry, I guess you know all about that, don't you?"

With a quick smile, I told her "no problem." I explained that in the short time I'd known Lizzy, I felt like I'd met my long-lost sister. And, really, Maggie and her family had made me feel so welcome. I felt horrible that Lizzy was stuck in the hospital because we had been careless in our investigation. I supposed that was partly why Donovan, et al, had warned us off so many times. Even I started to have second thoughts about this investigation.

Maggie and I went to the nurses' station and found out that Lizzy had just been cleared for visitors.

Maggie put her hand on my arm as we walked towards the Lizzy's room. "So, uh, Annie, who was that hunky guy you were talking to?" So she had noticed Donovan.

"Um, that's Donovan," I explained, turning bright red.

"Oh that's right. How could I have forgotten him! Oh, honey, Lizzy was right!" She beckoned for me to join her in visiting Lizzy. "He looks at you like you're a glass of water, and he's been in the desert for too, too long."

CHAPTER 22

FOR THE NEXT WEEK OR SO, WE settled into a routine of sorts. With Lizzy's arm out of commission, she couldn't work either as a bartender or a server at the Lighthouse Inn. Since I had some restaurant experience, and the restaurant got more business from curious people who wanted to see Lizzy and me, Kitty agreed to let me work Lizzy's shifts. I split the tips with Lizzy. Since we had a bodyguard at all times, Lizzy and I were kind of stuck together, so it was especially good to get out of the house and hang out at the Lighthouse Inn.

In fact, the only problem we had the whole week came in the form of Cindy. And it wasn't even "us" who had the problem—it was me. Kitty had let Lizzy into her office to take a quick catnap a few days into our new routine. Anyway, apparently, Cindy still held a grudge from the coffee-spilling incident (!!!) and transferred her anger from Lizzy to me. Or maybe she split it evenly. Every time she came to the bar to fill an order, she scowled at me. On this particular day of subbing for Lizzy, I was working behind the bar with George, who had gone on break. I resolved to find out why she detested us so much—it couldn't just be about spilt coffee, right?

"Here's my drink order," Cindy barked to me.

"Sure," I said, approaching the bar. After preparing her drinks, I seized the opportunity to talk to her.

"Say, uh, Cindy, can I talk to you for a sec?"

"What do you want?" she hissed. Yipe! I'd hate to meet her in a dark alley.

I cleared my throat nervously. Summoning up a little of the courage that let me quit CritiCentric so spectacularly, "Um, I'm really just trying to figure out what Lizzy and I did to piss you off so much."

Was it my imagination or did her eyes turn red? "What you did? Your very presence pisses me off!"

She flipped back her long blonde hair defiantly. Ugh! One of her hairs landed in a beer I had just poured for her table. "Um, Cindy? You, a, have a—"

She cut me off. "Do not even say my name!" Her voice lowered to a growly hiss. "In time you will be sorry for what you have done!" With that, she grabbed her tray and swept out of the bar area, rather imperiously, if you ask me. Also, and this was the really curious part, it sounded like her voice had slipped into a slight Greek-sounding accent.

Her accent reminded me of the case. The case that we hadn't worked on since the explosion. Or implosion? Meh, either way. Thankfully, we were both whole and mostly healthy after what happened, but I was starting to get anxious to find resolution. After all, I still had the jewels hidden away, plus the cops hadn't caught Harry's killer yet. Johnny Michaels had stopped by Lizzy's sister's a few days ago and notified Lizzy and me that Harry's killer was probably behind Joyce's death and the explosion. Since she had been in the explosion, they couldn't do an autopsy. However, when we told him that she was blue when we found her, he assumed cyanide poisoning too. He questioned me regarding the guys who swapped out my phone. I told him what I could about those slickster guys at the wine bar. A germ of an idea started in my brain. Lizzy and I needed to ditch our bodyguard soon to do some investigating.

Fortunately, during my confrontation with Cindy, our guard hadn't seen what happened. The second shift guard, Charlie Szablewski, probably loved the assignment more than the other two. He had benefitted the most when from guarding us. He enjoyed hanging out at the Lighthouse Inn while "babysitting" us; whereas, Donovan and the other guard were mostly limited to the Williams' house. And since Donovan insisted on taking the most dangerous shift—the early morning shift—I didn't get to see him. We had discovered that Charlie had a weakness for baseball; and given that his team was in the World Series, it seemed like a Win-Win. Especially since he got to work in a bar-slash-restaurant while watching over us. With him so focused on the game, I realized that Lizzy and I had the perfect way to get away from him, for at least a few hours.

"Is everything okay, Annie?" George asked cheerfully as he returned to the bar. "I just saw Cindy stomp out for a smoke. And I didn't mean to overhear," he added with a twinkle in his eyes, "but I could've sworn she was muttering your name and Lizzy's."

Frowning, I shrugged. George gently touched my shoulder. "Watch your back with her. I don't know why Kitty keeps her and Millicent on, but I do know that Cindy has a mean streak. I've heard stories of how Millicent tormented her peers at the same age. Cindy makes her look like Snow White. I'm just sayin'."

"A word to the wise and all that?" I gave him a tremulous smile. Why did I let Cindy get to me so much? I thought I had found backbone back when I confronted Tessa (which felt like another lifetime).

George laughed and lightly ruffled my hair, "I like you, kid. Just remember, don't let Cindy get your goat. Ignore her. Dig in, do your job, and let it go."

When Lizzy returned to work the next week, I found

myself disappointed that I had to stop doing it. While the regulars loved to see Lizzy back, I was loathe to quit working. I comforted myself with the fact that at least I would still get to hang out at the Lighthouse Inn while Lizzy worked.

At some point after Lizzy returned, we went down to Michigan City to get a new phone for me. After much finagling and a little bit of begging, I got my new phone. Unfortunately, I couldn't get any of my phone numbers, since my old phone was long-gone, thanks to the slicksters. However, I only needed one phone number. Before we made any more stops, I had to call Grandpa and Aunt Helen to make sure they knew I was safe. I was sure they had tried to call me a few times already.

I punched in their number, and let it ring. The phone rang and rang and rang. I left them a message that I was all right. I didn't say where I was, but I let them know that I was alive and out of town for a few days.

I still thought about my plans to get us investigating without our shadow. I hadn't talked to Lizzy about my plans—they were still formulating in my head. Then, out of blue, our investigation came to the forefront immediately and unexpectedly. Lizzy and I got an unexpected treat delivered to us a few days before Halloween.

After the crazy-busyness of the Halloween tourists over the past weekend, the Lighthouse Inn was practically dead. The dinner crowd was non-existent and only a few regulars, me, and our bodyguard sat at the bar. Almost the minute I got there, Lizzy said our pre-ordained code word. When the guard became a fixture in our lives, we designated the word "banana" to mean "I need to talk to you right away!"

Beckoning me to follow her, in the hallway Lizzy waved two tickets in front of my face. "Look what someone sent us!" She almost shouted it in her excitement but didn't want to attract the attention of our watchdog.

Lowering her voice to a whisper, she pulled me into the bar's storage area. "Seriously, check out these Haunted Tour tickets! This will be really fun and should take our minds off of this stalemate." She handed me the tickets.

"Who sent them?" Taking the tickets, I looked closely at them. I don't know what I expected to find. A hidden code on the tickets? A spot of dirt on the tickets that could only come from the clay dirt in a specific part of Brook Harbor? Whatever it was, I didn't see it.

"That's really cool. I hope you have fun," I said dejectedly, handing her back the tickets.

"Oh, we will-… Wait, why aren't you going?"

I jerked my thumb back at Mr. Baseball. "When is it? How can you even go? I'm assuming it's a nighttime event. And before Friday, right? I mean, Friday is Halloween. And, let me count... Wednesday, Thursday, Friday. That's only two days away!"

Lizzy made a "Pish" gesture at me. We both knew that as one of Kitty's best friends, Kitty would probably give her the time off—even last minute.

Lizzy added, "But to answer your first question, the tickets are for Thursday!" Then she proceeded to make a scary "Woooo!" sound, presumably to get me in the mood for Halloween. I wasn't big on Halloween but was intrigued by a Haunted Tour.

"Crap! So it's tomorrow night. I really want to go... oh, if only we could lose my shadow. Why oh why did we let Donovan saddle us with this guy?"

"Humpf! Us?" Lizzy laughed as we walked back to the bar area. "We are saddled, but we can get away if we really want to badly enough." She winked at me and added in a whisper, "Besides, I have a plan. When we get home tonight, I'll tell you all about it."

Later that night, Lizzy, her sister, and I were hunched over Maggie's kitchen table at one in the morning, putting the final touches on Lizzy's plan to get us away from our shadow. Seriously! We just wanted to have some fun! Was that too much to ask? They switched shifts every eight hours. Our little party conveniently broke up before Donovan started his shift of guarding us at two a.m.

I agreed willingly to the deception we were about to do to the poor guard. Poor guard, what am I saying? This illusion we were creating had more to do with smoke and mirrors, disguised as beer, pizza, and Game 7 of the World Series.

Charlie, Lizzy, and I got to the bar about an hour before the game started. Lizzy and I had an hour and a half to put our plan in motion and get to the starting point for the Haunted Tour. Lizzy filled George in on the plan, since we would need his help.

"Naturally, anything for my little sweetie-pies," George said, as reported by Lizzy. She texted me a "thumbs-up" and "Operation Distract Charlie can begin."

We figured that, with George's help, we could plant Charlie at the bar to watch Game 7 of the World Series. Since, the teams were tied at three apiece, I knew he would be focused. After getting Charlie settled with his non-alcohol beer and pizza, Lizzy and I slipped out the back door. I crossed my fingers that the Tigers played well, which would easily buy us more time.

"Who do you think sent us the tickets?" I asked Lizzy as we clambered into her truck.

"Beats me, but isn't it awesome that they did? Maybe it's some weird admirers after what happened last week." Lizzy shrugged it off. She was probably right, too. We had gotten a few odd gifts delivered to us at the Lighthouse Inn. What is that saying? Oh, yes, don't look a gift horse in the mouth.

We got to the start of the tour in Turtle Bay just in time. Apparently, it was a walking tour of the older homes in downtown Turtle Bay. The crisp night air and dark sky above really added to the atmosphere.

The tour guide played his part well, too. Dressed like Vincent Price from the classic horror movie, Fall of the

House of Usher, he greeted us all with an affected accent, "Welcome to the Haunted Tour of Turtle Bay's Historical Homes," and proceeded to explain how the tour would go. In the next two hours, we would go through five of the most haunted homes in Turtle Bay.

The tour began in an old Victorian home that stood slightly back from the main drag. Eerie lights shone throughout the house as the tour guide explained the ghost situation. He recounted a tale of lives lost through a shipwreck in the bay and a Typhoid outbreak. Lizzy grabbed my arm, causing me to jump about two feet high.

"I think I saw something!" she whispered in my ear, still clutching my arm.

Slapping her hand away, I said, "No way. You're just affected by the atmosphere. C'mon, Lizzy."

And on we went like that throughout the Painted Lady and at the next stop, an old Cape Cod house across the street. Once or twice, I thought I saw something out of the corner of my eye, too, but I didn't want to feed into Lizzy's nerves.

At our third stop, which was a few "doors" down... our tour guide took us to a cemetery. On the cemetery grounds was a little caretaker's house that was supposed to be haunted. The house looked the most haunted of all of them. For a caretaker's house, it didn't look much cared-for through the ages. In the dark, the little house (which was barely more than a two-story shack) looked dark grey. The shutters were falling off, and the porch looked like if one stepped on it, one might go through it. A shiver went through me.

"Did you hear that?" Lizzy broke into my thoughts.

"For the umpteenth time, no! For goodness' sake, Lizzy, we are on a ghost tour! You should expect to see ghosts!"

"Bah! You're no fun! Being scared is part of the fun. Any ninny knows that." Lizzy moved ahead of me, clearly in a snit.

Somehow, the dark got a little darker as I walked on, alone. "Oof!" I exclaimed as I tripped over a gravestone. "Lizzy? Are you there?" I couldn't even see her anymore. OK, now I regretted pooh-poohing her fears as my anxiety increased.

I couldn't see much more than my hands in front of my face. I thought the entire tour had left me in the dust.

Behind me, I heard a twig snap. I turned around quickly but couldn't see anything because of the dark. I was able to make out the silhouette of a tree, but... I rubbed my eyes. Was that tree moving? Was that tree moving towards me? Oh my gosh! I screamed as the tree got closer and... shushed me. Wait, shushed me?

"Shush, Annie! It's just me, Donovan!"

"Wow, you really freaked me out!" I was shaking all over and could feel my heart pounding.

"Sorry. Hey—where's Lizzy?"

"You're not mad I gave Charlie the slip?" I looked up at him skeptically.

"We'll get to that in a minute."

"Oh." Nervously, I licked my lips.

Donovan's eyebrows shot up to his hairline. He moaned a little. "Please don't do that. This is serious business."

"Don't do what?" I asked, innocently. I had no idea what he meant. I bit my bottom lip in consternation.

"Or that! You have no idea what you're doing to me, do you?"

"Frankly, Donovan, I'd appreciate it if you'd stop talking in riddles and help me find Lizzy and the rest of the tour."

"Yeah, that's a good plan. How'd you get separated from the group anyway?"

Suddenly, my mouth dropped open and all I could do was point towards the second floor of the caretaker's shack. I felt my eyes become as wide as saucers. I gripped Donovan's arm with my other hand.

"Annie, what is it?"

"I-I-I," All I could do was point.

Donovan followed my gaze.

"Oh wow! Did you see that? Is there supposed to be anyone up there?"

I gulped and shook my head. "Th-the t-t-tour guide," I paused to gather my thoughts and stop shaking. "Okay, the tour guide said that shack hadn't been lived in for more than 20 years!"

"So, no blondes in gauzy white dresses currently reside there?" Donovan asked. I couldn't tell if he was mocking me or not.

"I don't think so. But look!" I started shaking again. "I did see a blonde woman, I think."

I heard him roll his eyes; however, he humored me. "Well, let's go check it out."

At that moment, Lizzy came racing back. "Annie, where were you? I thought you were behind me. Oh, Donovan, hi. How did you find us?"

"You left a trail of breadcrumbs," he said wryly, lifting an eyebrow.

"We left a tra—? Oh, good one!"

"Lizzy, we can't talk! We have to go to that shack ahead. Look at the window!"

"What window?"

I pointed to the second story window. "Now she's gone! You know, I know this is kind of far-fetched, but she matched Marcos' description of his wife."

"Wife? Whose wife? What are you guys talking about?" Lizzy looked from me to Donovan, and back again. "What did I miss? Crap! I miss all the fun stuff!" She stomped her foot in protest.

"Actually, you're just in time to see some fun stuff, as you put it," Donovan said. "We're going ghost hunting."

"We are? Goody!"

"Oh no."

Lizzy and I said that simultaneously. I will leave it to

my dear reader to determine who said what.

"That thing," I said, pointing the dilapidated shack. "That building—it doesn't look like it could support three people going in," I said, trying to get out of our ghost hunting expedition. The problem wasn't that I didn't believe in ghosts; the problem was that I did. And as proven by our adventure at Joyce's, I think I've shown ghosts freak me out a little bit.

"Good point, Annie. You and I can go in. Lizzy, can you guard the door?"

Apparently, Donovan didn't read into subtext right then.

"To make sure the apparition doesn't leave?"

"Do you really think it was a ghost, Lizzy?"

"Hunh? Then what was it?"

Donovan seemed to like answering questions with questions, "How did you get these tour tickets again? Never mind, don't answer that right now."

Grabbing my hand (oh okay, now I could see the worth in this adventure), he dragged me across a few cemetery plots to the ramshackle building. His warm hand felt good holding mine, helping me feel calmer. I no longer felt that scared going into the building.

Until I saw a bat fly out of the front door. "Was that a b-b-bat?" Oh my gosh, why did it always have to be bats?

"Yeah, are you gonna let a little bat scare you?" I saw the glistening white of Donovan's teeth as he smiled. Suddenly, I felt silly. After all, the bat was probably more afraid of me.

I shook my head as we entered the building. Donovan clicked on his flashlight.

"You've had a flashlight this whole time? Why didn't you use it?" I let go of his hand and held onto the stair rail as we headed upstairs. It seemed like each step creaked.

Ignoring my questioning, we continued upward. He shined the flashlight on the window we had seen from the outside. We saw an old table in front of the window. A broken antique lamp stood on an old yellowed doily on the table. Donovan quickly shined the light on it. As he moved the light, I thought I saw something that looked out of place on the table. Donovan had already moved down the hallway and was trying doors. There was no sign of the woman—it was as though she had disappeared into thin air.

"Wait! Donovan! Bring that light back here."

"I'm on my way." I heard his footsteps get louder again. I ran my fingers along the table very gingerly. Some moonlight shined through the window. Just before he returned with the flashlight, my fingers found a thick piece of paper. The paper felt like good stationery paper and smelled like… what did it smell like? I had the smell before. But I couldn't place where. Donovan broke into my thoughts.

"Annie, what are you holding?"

"Oh, right," Donovan's voice brought me back to the present. I wished I could place that smell. "This piece of paper was on the table. Read it with me."

I read it, with Donovan peering over my shoulder. The note said:

Find Marcos. Find the murderer.

"Oh wow, Donovan! A real clue!"

"Hold on, hold on, Annie. Let's step back from this for a minute."

"But that must mean that woman we saw definitely was not a ghost. She must have written this note!"

"Perhaps, but—"

My thoughts were coming pretty fast now, and I cut him off. "Do you think it could've been Tina Delvecchio?"

"We have to get out of here. Now! I need to get you and Lizzy back to her sister's place. For the next several days, can you promise me to not leave her sister's place?" We walked downstairs as we spoke. "Did you ever replace that phone that was used as a detonator?"

"I did," and to demonstrate, I pulled it out of my pocket.

"Nice phone. Mind if I look at it for a minute?"

"Um, sure, okay," I hesitated slightly.

"Did you, uh, get any apps or internet or anything with it?"

"I think so. I haven't really had a chance to play with it."

Donovan fiddled with some of the keys while I waited, not so patiently. When I started to fidget, Donovan gave my phone back to me.

"Is Lizzy under house arrest too?" I asked, accepting the phone. Okay, I'll admit I was being a bit snotty, but I was getting tired of being treated like we did something wrong. Seriously.

Donovan sighed, "Annie, you know it isn't like that, right? I mean, this is just for your safety. It's because I care."

Our eyes made contact as he spoke. I licked my lips again. I felt his arm circle my waist and pull me closer. I closed my eyes in expectation, then, poof. Nothing but air.

"So, did you find anything?" Lizzy asked, bounding up to us. She quickly realized what was going on. "Oops, sorry. Wow, would you look at the time? I think I'll go for a little walk."

I put my hand on Lizzy's sleeve. "It's okay." The mood was broken anyhow. Donovan and I shared a regretful look over the interruption, but at least his level of interest was coming into focus.

Donovan filled Lizzy on the note and made her promise to stick close to her sister's place. He relented and said she could go to work, but the bodyguard had to stay with us. He wanted us to stick together, so I kept going to work with Lizzy.

Donovan thought I'd be safe. Little did he know.

CHAPTER 23

S O, THE NEXT DAY FOUND ME AT work with Lizzy and a new bodyguard. This new guy stood post by the front door. He told Lizzy and I that he needed to watch all comings and goings, and make sure we weren't gone from the bar and restaurant areas for too long. Amazingly enough, Kitty agreed with this. I say it was amazing because the guy looked pretty intimidating. Even with the colder weather outside, he wore short sleeves as he stood by the door. His arms looked like trees, and I wasn't sure he had a neck. But I felt a little safer; I think Lizzy did too.

Since Lizzy worked the lunch and dinner shifts, I made myself comfortable at the bar with a book. Lizzy and I chatted when we could (in other words, when there were no other bar patrons) and she kept me full of diet soda. In return, I helped Lizzy replace a keg of beer, since George had the day off. The day went by pretty quickly, and the evening promised to go by just as fast. Since it was a weeknight, the bar wouldn't be too busy, and Kitty had promised that we'd probably get to go home at nine o'clock.

An hour before it was time to go, I was in the

stockroom, gathering up bottles of beer for Lizzy to restock the bar. I figured if I could help her with her closing duties ahead of time, we'd be able to leave that much faster.

Imagine my surprise when Cindy Devlin approached me in the stockroom. We had barely spoken after she freaked out a few days ago. Her face looked weird and, initially, I couldn't figure out why. Suddenly, I realized that she was smiling, and I had never seen her smile before. Interesting. She was one of the few people I'd ever seen who did not look better smiling. Usually a smile made someone more attractive. A smile on her looked uncomfortable and almost grotesque.

But she was smiling. I'd take that over a scowl any day.

"Hello, Annie!" she exclaimed as she came up to me.

I smiled back, and said, "Hi Cindy. How are you?"

"I'm good. Look, I just wanted to talk to you for a minute. You know how I've been not-so-nice to you and Lizzy?"

Wanting to be polite, I downplayed it, "Oh no, no. You've been fine. Really."

"You and I both know I haven't been fine. I've been horrid to you." I was so shocked, I almost dropped the bottle of beer in my hand. Gingerly, I put the beer down in the bus tub I was using. My surprise didn't end there. Cindy held out her hand for me to shake. "Do you forgive me? Shall we let bygones be bygones?"

"Of course! I would like it if we could be friends." I shook hands with her and felt a slight prick of pain on the side of my pinky. Too late, I pulled back my hand, and cried, "Ouch!"

"Oh, I'm sorry, it must be this needle I just pricked you with," Cindy said, still with that crazy smile. Except now, two of her smiled at me. I stumbled a bit on my feet. "Come on, Annie, let's get you out of here. I think you could use some fresh air." Cindy put her arm around me like we were old pals. She bundled me out the back door to a waiting black sedan. In my foggy state, I thought two things: nothing good ever happens in black sedans and was it my imagination, or did Cindy have an accent all of a sudden? Then everything went dark.

•••

When I awoke, I discovered my hands and feet were bound. They had covered my mouth, too. I could taste the duct tape. Gross. I could tell we were moving, but it was totally dark, and I could only hear muffled voices. It felt like we were moving on the water. I could smell water and stale cigars. Besides being distracted by the nasty duct tape taste (seriously, it was bad), I thought, "Where are they taking me? And, why oh why didn't I listen to Donovan?" before I lost consciousness again.

I woke up again to the sound of gently lapping waves. So, I was definitely on water; hearing seagulls squawking overhead clinched it. Some sunlight snuck through broken Venetian blinds. Depending on which way the room faced, I figured it must be morning. I took an assessment of the room. The ugliest moss green couch sat under a velvet painting of cats playing poker. Hmmm, an interesting take on tacky chic, I thought. My ears perked up.

"…and then I want you to find out whatever she knows and if she won't talk, then I want you to…"

I strained to hear the rest of it, but only heard their footsteps going away from the door. That voice, though. Two things surprised me: it was definitely a woman's voice, and I vaguely recognized it. Suddenly one set of footsteps got louder again. At the sound of the door opening, I closed my eyes to feign sleep.

"Hey, hey you, wake up," a man said in a thick Eastern European accent, poking me on the shoulder. "We didn't give you that much sedative."

I did my best to appear groggy, which actually wasn't that hard. My head felt like someone had smacked it with a baseball bat. Wow, maybe it was a metal bat, the way my head hurt.

"Annie Malone, why have you been poking your cute little nose where it doesn't belong, eh? We warned you plenty of times."

Even though my head must have weighed a million pounds and my bindings held me tight, I tried to sit up, but failed. I decided to moan instead; I had earned it. After I had moaned for a minute or so, my genius captor realized I couldn't talk with the duct tape over my mouth.

"Oh yeah, right, I suppose you need me to remove this," he said, right before he ripped it off. I spit on him immediately.

"Hey, what was that for?" the thug asked, rather stupidly, in my opinion. Which prompted me to spit at him again.

Wiping his face, he uttered a horrific curse through a soiled bandanna. He threatened me, "You do that one more time, I'm putting that tape back on."

I just scowled at him. While I needed to get the upperhand, I found myself at a distinct disadvantage. I figured a good, scowling silence might freak him out a little.

"Now, I'm gonna repeat my question, Annie Malone—that is your name, correct?" I curtly nodded. He continued, "Why have you been poking your nose unnecessarily around this business of Marcos and Harry?"

"What do you want with me anyway?"

"We know you have them. Where are they?"

"Have what?" I knew he meant the gems. I figured if I played dumb, I could get him to talk more and stay alive a little longer. Although, my heart sunk a little when I realized that no one knew where I was. I didn't even know where I was.

Suddenly, a redheaded woman walked in the room with the agility of a cat. She actually wore a very tight leather outfit. Kinda like Cat woman, actually. Her face looked familiar, but I didn't know who she was until I heard her speak. "Annie, dear Annie. We need you to tell us where you hid them!"

"You! Cindy Devlin!" I spit at her. She promptly slapped me across the face. Her thug took a step backwards.

"Why oh why did you and your stupid friend get involved with this issue? What good is in it for you?"

Remember my theory on bravery and stupidity having a very thin line between them? I was walking that very thin as I sat there, bound up, and wondering how anyone would even find me. With a bravado that I certainly didn't feel, I retorted, "What good is in it for me? I was trying to clear my name and find Harry's killer."

"Don't treat me like I'm stupid." She slapped me again.

"Hey! What was that for?"

"I knew what you were doing. But you got in the way of our organization!"

"So, how does Marcos figure into this organization?" I fully expected to see panic in her eyes at his name. Assuming he was the kingpin, I expected to see fear. Instead, she laughed.

"Dear Marcos. We made him disappear." She callously snapped her fingers. I tried not to flinch at this news. Now it looked like I'd never get to meet him.

"Who do you work for then?"

"Don't you mean to say, 'who works for you then?'?"

"You're the 'kingpin'? You're the boss? So, if you're the Big Bad Boss Lady, who is Tina Delvecchio? How does she figure into this?"

"Ah, dear Tina. Yes, she has been a thorn in our side for years." I couldn't figure out if she was using the royal "we" or if there were additional people involved. Since she had said "organization," I decided to go with multiple people.

"But why? What is her role? If you are, indeed, the Head Honcho?" I said as I started to laugh. I must admit, finding out Cindy was the boss made me feel braver. She still intimidated me, but there was a certain familiarity.

"How dare you laugh! We have been successful in trafficking multiple things!"

"Like jewels?"

I finally got a look of surprise from her, then a knowing gleam. "So you do have the gems. I knew it. Where are they?"

"That's for me to know and you to find out!"

Cindy's thug took a step forward. She held up her hand. "No, no Alex. Don't hurt her yet." Then, to me, she said, "Tsk tsk tsk, angering me is one thing. You do not want to anger Alex." Alex scowled at me in response. To be honest, I wasn't sure if he really scowled or if that was his permanent face. She gave an exaggerated sigh. "After all, he carries all my guns. I don't like to ruin the line of my outfit." She ran her hand down her size 2 torso.

I had to admit she did have an enviable figure. All that running in cold weather must pay off. As any woman knows, this was my opportunity to make my biggest mark, "Oh, you don't need a gun to ruin your line, Cindy."

Cindy frowned at me, and asked, "What do you mean?"

"Well, I don't mean to be so indelicate as to mention it, *dear*. But it looks like you might you might have eaten one too many chocolate chip muffins."

Bingo! I didn't even have time to smirk before she lunged at me. Knocking over my chair, she pinned me on the ground and spit at me. "That is from me!" Then she spit again. "And that is for my Mother!"

Restricted in my movements, I could only move my head from side to side to avoid her DNA all over my face. Trying to keep my mouth closed, I mumbled, "Who is your Mother?"

"Tina Delvecchio!" And she spit at me again. She got in one more hard slap across my face and got up. Still tied to the chair, I lay on the floor awaiting their next plan. "But she is worthless! I was raised by my Father in Greece and learned his business well!"

I couldn't see Tina and Alex talking behind me, but I heard hushed voices discussing my fate. I tried to twist my head around to see them, but my angle was all wrong.

Alex came back and put the duct tape back over my mouth. Still on the chair, he began to drag me across the room. I had no idea where they were taking me, but I heard a helicopter overhead.

"Oh, good, Alex, our helicopter is arriving. Once we get out of here, we can take Annie into Canada, and no one's the wiser."

"What about the jewels, Ma'am?"

"I guess we'll just have to cut our losses. This region has gotten too dangerous. But we must be sure to take her. No one will miss a little nobody failure, anyway."

Ouch.

"I guess we can either dump her out over Lake Michigan." After the helicopter, we heard footsteps.

Suddenly, we heard shouts outside the door. It sounded like a scuffle.

Cindy held up her hand, lightly laughing, and said, "Well, well, Alex, it sounds like the boys are fighting again."

Alex began to simper in a way that can only be described as creepy, "Can I push her out of the helicopter, Ma'am?"

"Yes, Alex. You are such a pet." She actually reached up and patted her toady on the head. Ugh. It was all I could do to not throw up in my duct tape. At least their weirdness distracted me from panicking.

The door opened and a slightly disheveled Donovan entered the room, guns a' blazing. And he was backed by armed officers. Stampeding into the room, they made quick work of Cindy and Alex. I found out later that they had also quickly made work of the armed guards who stood outside my prison.

Quickly untying me, Donovan checked my pulse and my eyes to make sure I was okay.

"Pees remuv dah tabe!" After he freed my hands, I pointed to my duct taped mouth.

Determining that I was fine, Donovan decided to gently tease me, asking, "I'm sorry, what are you trying to say? I can't hear you with that tape over your mouth." Crinkles appeared at the corners of his eyes when he smiled down at me. "Okay, okay. Quick or slow?"

"Kik." Riiipppp!

"Ouch!"

"You said quick," Donovan picked me up off the chair and held me close. "Let's make sure we don't have to go through that again!"

I snuggled close to him. "My hero! How did you ever find me?"

"Before I tell you, I'd to introduce you to some people. Are you free for dinner tonight?"

"What is today anyway?"

"You haven't been out that long."

"So, today is Saturday?"

"You got it!"

"I can do dinner, definitely. Is this our first date?" I batted my eyes flirtatiously at him.

"Well, quite a few people will be joining us. Kitty vowed that if I brought you back safely, she would kill the fatted calf and put on a shindig the likes of which Brook Harbor has never seen. I was hoping you'd let me escort one of the Guests of Honor."

"Who's the other?"

He jokingly zipped his mouth. Carrying me to the helicopter, he strapped me into my seat and got himself comfortable. "But I hope it's the first of many, many dates, darling Annie."

Swoon.

CHAPTER 24

A T SEVEN THAT NIGHT, Maggie and Nick's doorbell rang. I ran to the door before anyone could beat me to it. Seeing Donovan at the door, I called back to the Williamses that I'd see them at the Lighthouse shortly.

As I was about to open the door, Donovan had his hand primed to knock on it. Had I been made taller, he would have knocked my forehead; he knocked air instead. I stifled a nervous giggle as I walked with him out to his Jeep. Beneath my serviceable old barn jacket, I had changed into the peacock blue sweater he had seen me modeling at Janie's shop and a black pencil skirt. I thought my black peek-a-boo toe shoes really completed the outfit.

Donovan wore a navy blue shirt and blue jeans, with a grey sports jacket. And he held out a bouquet of red tulips.

"Oh, aren't those beautiful!" I exclaimed, taking his offered arm. "No one has ever gotten me flowers before! I love them!"

"You're kidding me, right?"

"Nope. Well, I take that back. I got a small bouquet of roses for a school dance once. But all of the heads popped off by the time the night was over. I think I kept catching the flowers on door frames."

I caught Donovan looking at me fondly. Blushing, I said, "What?"

"Nothing. You must be really happy, though. You are practically vibrating from excitement."

"I know," I said, my blush deepening. "I've always had a tough time restraining my joy. I'm really looking forward to this."

•••

When we arrived at the Lighthouse, almost everyone I'd met in the past few weeks was in the bar and restaurant. Kitty had set up an amazing buffet. And she wasn't kidding about the "fatted calf." She had enough beef tenderloin available to feed an army.

"So, ahem, here's dessert too."

"French silk pie! My favorite! How did Kitty know?"

"Kitty didn't, it was my suggestion," Donovan winked. "It's my favorite, too."

Donovan escorted me around the room where people kept slapping me on the back and congratulating me.

Out of the side of my mouth, I said to Donovan, "Why do they keep congratulating me? I know I survived a trauma, but I hardly deserve congratulations."

Donovan looked at me in shock. "You don't know, do you?"

"Donovan!" A strange man approached Donovan. His voice was definitely familiar... and looking closely, I detected a strong resemblance to a young Abe Vigoda. Abe Vigoda! The proverbial light went off in my head. "How the heck are you? I finally made it! Wow! This is quite a party."

Donovan grabbed the hand the man offered, and turned to me, "Annie, I'd like you to meet the other Guest of Honor, Marcos Landrostassis. Marcos, this is Annie Malone."

A smile broke out over Marcos' face, "Annie! So good to meet you in person!"

I had almost convinced myself that Marcos didn't exist, yet here the man stood in front of me. "You are real! You have no idea how nice it is to meet you! But what is this? Why are you here, too?"

"Annie, Marcos hired me as a private investigator for this job. He has been undercover for years. He had done some time in prison many years ago and they cut him a deal. He just needed to infiltrate Cindy's organization."

"But Cindy's so young. She can't have been the head of it for very long." I scrunched up my face trying to do math in my head.

"She wasn't. You know her mother is Tina Delvecchio. What you don't know is her father was the infamous Dmitri Tasios."

"He was her father? So, being an outlaw is in her genes?"

Marcos laughed at my little joke while Donovan smiled indulgently. "You could say that."

"Oh, Annie! You are a treasure. Donovan, hold on to this one. She has the patience of a saint. Even when I yelled at her over the phone, she put up with me." He slapped me on the back so hard, I almost fell down. Donovan steadied me, saying, "Easy there, Marcos. She's not used to our rougher ways."

I smiled up at the men, "Oh, I'm fine. Hey, there's that blonde woman we saw at the haunted house! What's she doing here?"

"Oh, that's right, Annie, you haven't met Diana yet," Marcos exclaimed and briefly left us to bring Diana to meet me.

"You must be Annie," Diana said with a sweetly soft voice. "It is so nice to meet you. I have so wanted to meet you."

"It's nice to meet you too! But why didn't you introduce yourself earlier? We saw you at that house across from Effie, didn't we?"

She nodded, "Yes, you did. I'm so sorry about that. I'm also sorry about Lizzy falling into that pit. And breaking her arm. I was so relieved when you escaped that exploding house, though. If I had known they had swapped out your phone…"

Donovan's eyebrows shot up. "Lizzy fell into a pit! This is a story I must hear!"

"What must you hear?" Lizzy joined us at that exact moment. Donovan made all of the introductions, which Lizzy took in stride. "So, you are the blonde we kept seeing?"

"Yep. Marcos had asked me to kind of keep an eye on you. He knew what had happened to Harry, so he went into hiding while the gang regrouped. Between myself and Donovan, I think we had our hands full keeping you two safe." I bristled a little bit at that comment, but I suppose she had a point. Lizzy and I did seem to attract trouble.

Donovan directed us towards a table and left to grab us all drinks and food. I got up to join them, and he motioned me down. "Let Marcos and Diana tell you their story." I smiled and nodded.

So, Marcos and Diana put all of the pieces of the story together for me. Marcos started first, "About six years ago, an unnamed law enforcement agency called me in for a special project. I had gotten involved with some bad stuff as a young man, and they were giving me an opportunity to wipe the slate clean. They had a lead on the head of an International Crime Organization, but they couldn't pin him down. The guy was based out of the U.S., but he could easily move around. He was like a chameleon."

"Has anyone ever seen him?"

"Had, you mean. He passed away a few years ago." Marcos gave a little laugh. "I had forgotten how much you liked to interrupt with questions."

"Sorry." Embarrassed at my faux pas, I looked down.

"Hey, Annie, don't worry about it. I'm just joking with

you. I felt bad when you were interviewing me. I knew I had to pretend to be one way, it really... ach, it doesn't matter anymore. Anyway, yeah, this guy was hard to catch. And, he had his grubby paws in everything! So, they wanted me to go deep undercover. Originally, Diana wasn't supposed to come up with me, but I pitched a fit. I told them I wouldn't come up, that all of the contacts and connections I had made would be nothing, because I needed to have Diana with me. So, we moved up here.

"For the first couple of years, they had me do little crimes to prove myself to the group. Then, about two years ago, they invited me on as the head of their Gems Division."

"Did you actually steal the jewels?"

"No, underlings did that part. Actually, Harry was one of our best mules."

"But what I don't get is, why the book? I mean, weren't you trying to keep a low profile?"

"That's just it, with Harry's business, it seemed like a reasonable project to start. That way, his frequent trips up here would be explained. But then, Harry got killed and you got blamed. And I went into hiding."

"Wait a minute! Are you the one who got me off the hook when Chad Dupah was questioning me?"

"I can't stand that guy. You seemed like too nice a kid to get questioned by that jerk."

"Thanks, but how did you know I was even at the police station?"

"Donovan told me. Back when I first went deep undercover, we had set up a complicated (but fast) method of communication. I could tell he was starting to have feelings for you even then."

"He was?" At that moment, the subject of the conversation came back laden with a tray of drinks and a plate of appetizers.

"Did I miss anything?" Donovan asked. I looked over at Marcos, who conspiratorially winked at me.

"Okay, so why was Harry killed then?"

"My guess is he had done something to displease 'Her Majesty.'"

"Her Majesty?"

"I'm sorry, I meant Cindy. When she took over from her father, right after he made me head of jewel thefts, she changed quite a few things. She started making us more visible. Harry felt uncomfortable about it. He also felt uneasy about his business being used by this side business. He had business partners to deal with and worried that there could be problems. As it turns out, he was right.

"On that ill-fated Saturday night, Cindy crept up to his room after her shift at the Lighthouse. She was just going to talk to him, try to keep him with the organization. But he was insistent on leaving. So, she left, but she didn't leave the building. She stayed in the shadows until Harry drew his bath. After he got in the tub, she tried to reason with him again. However, this time she brought hardware with her."

"A gun?"

Marcos nodded. "Poor guy didn't have a chance. And, of course, you happened upon the body."

"How do you know all this?"

"Diana had been following Cindy."

"Diana?"

"Yeah, she's been a huge help on this case. She couldn't really get a regular job up here. Since I was undercover and all, she bided her time making inroads with the more delicate aspects of the organization. She's been my eyes and ears. Thanks, honey."

"Don't mention it, babe." Marcos kissed Diana soundly, then Diana took over the story.

"When Marcos went into hiding, as I've mentioned, I kept an eye on you both." Again, Diana gestured to Lizzy and me. "Please don't be offended. I felt it was my duty to Marcos. Annie, he felt responsible for the mess you were in. But he couldn't tell anybody without jeopardizing years and years of work."

"Was that you who sent us the Haunted House Guided Tour tickets?" This time it was Lizzy who interrupted. "And, who killed Joyce?"

Diana smiled at her, "It was. I figured it would be a fun outing for you both, and I knew you would be able to give your bodyguard the slip. Unfortunately, Joyce had seen too much. Apparently, Cindy overhead the arrangements you had made to talk to her and got to her first. They slipped her some cyanide. Well, and blew up her house. But, as you know, the cyanide killed her before her house got blown up."

"That's too bad. I'm sorry that Joyce paid the price for trying to help us. And about the bodyguards, Donovan," I said, turning to Donovan. "I know that private investigators and law enforcement agencies don't give people a bodyguard if they are just normal people. How did regular old Lizzy and I get bodyguards?"

Donovan looked at us rather sheepishly. "I paid for your guards personally." He ran his fingers through his hair. "I'm sorry if it seems presumptuous that I did that. I just knew who we were dealing with, and I was worried about you and Lizzy."

"Also, how did you find me? Where had they taken me again? To Washington Island, which is pretty far north?"

"When you got your new phone... well, do you remember when I was looking at it?" I nodded. "I activated your GPS function. You're not mad, are you? I just knew that you and Lizzy would rush madly into where angels fear to tread."

"I guess it's better to be safe than sorry. And your fears do appear to have been well-founded. So, I'm not mad. Are you mad, Lizzy?"

"I'm only mad that my drink is dead," Lizzy said before she got up to get another cocktail.

"Marcos, isn't that Ed Peters?" Diana said, getting up. "Excuse us, please. Honey, we really should go say hi to him."

"I'm right behind you." Marcos got up too, and, suddenly, Donovan and I were alone at the table.

I dimpled as I smiled at him.

"It should be against the law when you do that," Donovan said.

"Do what?" I asked innocently. I smiled a little more.

"Okay, before you drive me completely distracted. There's a couple of things I need to talk to you about."

Here it comes. He's going to tell me about the wife he has locked in the attic.

"By the way, Annie, what are your plans now that the book is definitely defunct?"

"Well, I have that bonus Harry gave me, so I can pay off some bills and put the rest in the bank. Then I guess I'll take Kitty up on her offer of working here at the Lighthouse."

"So, you're going to stay up here?"

"I am. What are your plans? I suppose as a private investigator you'd get more work in a bigger city." I couldn't help but be sad at that thought. I had really grown to like Donovan and wanted to see where things would go.

"Are you trying to get rid of me?" He smiled. "Actually, much like you, I'm starting to really like Door County." Somehow, I knew he didn't really mean Door County.

"And?"

"And, I'm going to stay too. Maybe I really will become an insurance agent." He grinned down at me.

All I could do was smile, before I remembered, "Hey, you said a couple of things. What else did you want to discuss?"

"Cindy Devlin (which was an alias of Cynthia Tasios) had a bounty on her head, dead or alive."

"A bounty? And did she really think 'Cindy' was an effective alias for 'Cynthia'? It's the same name! It's like saying 'Jackie' is an alias for 'Jacqueline.' She wasn't really that bright, was she?"

Donovan cleared his throat, and continued, "Well, it would seem that the reward was significant."

"How significant?"

"Five hundred thousand dollars."

"And you are telling me this because…"

"You and Lizzy kind of caught her. I mean Marcos did a lot of the legwork, but he wants to split it with you and Lizzy. Besides, you were the one who got the confession out of her, right?"

"Yeah." I could barely speak. Donovan took advantage of the situation to give me a kiss that curled my toes. Mmmm… I was definitely starting to like Door County, too.

ABOUT THE AUTHOR

Jacqueline lives in the beautiful state of Wisconsin, where it is fairly common to experience all four seasons in just one day. When not writing, she loves to draw, paint, bike, hike, read, and tweak recipes. She would rather be outside than indoors, hanging out with family and friends.

Made in the USA
Middletown, DE
07 April 2022

63727092R00126